WHAT COMES AFTER DAWN

A MYNART MYSTERY THRILLER
BOOK 5

ADDISON MICHAEL

PAGES & PIE PUBLISHING
♦ Author Services ♦

2023 Pages & Pie Publishing

ISBN: 979-8-9862920-6-9

Library of Congress Catalogue-in-Publication Data

Michael, Addison

What comes after dawn: a mynart mystery thriller / Addison Michael

Cover Design by Art by Karri

Editing by Tiffany Avery and Sarah Malone

While set in real places, this novel is a work of fiction. All characters, events, and police agencies portrayed are products of the author's imagination. Any resemblance to established practices or similarity that may depict actual people, either alive or deceased, are entirely fictional and purely coincidental.

www.addisonmichael.com

For my book club readers—you know who you are
Thanks for your support

PROLOGUE
MINA

The mangled dead body lay on a cold, steel slab at the morgue. She knew the temperature could not be higher than a frigid forty degrees Fahrenheit. She was wrapped in a long black peacoat, so she didn't feel the cold. The dimly lit room was sterile and held the vibe of a hospital room, save the lifeless corpse that lay in front of her. Morgues didn't bother her. She had always been able to view a body without emotion. Until today.

A single light bulb in the middle of the room flickered.

"Creepy," she acknowledged while looking up, but not even that creeped her out. She turned her attention back to the reason she was in the morgue.

He was uncovered. She could see that his right kneecap was grotesquely swollen and misplaced. The lower half of the leg was bent and twisted up next to his body at an unnatural angle. At first, she viewed him in the same emotionless, clinical way she had viewed other bodies in the past. As a former crime analyst, it had been necessary to assess a body here and there for clues others might have missed.

Several bones were broken to enable his leg to twist the way it did. His neck was positioned at an odd angle. One arm dangled lifelessly over the side of the table. She chose not to look at the back of his skull. His skull was the place where he'd received the most damage. His head had likely bounced off the pavement after impact. Bruises and swelling made his face almost impossible to identify. Almost.

But she'd know him anywhere. He was fit for his age. He was an older man, but this had only made him more attractive to her. His arms showed muscle tone. His stomach was flat. His physical appearance never mattered to her much, though. All that mattered now was this was the body of her one true love.

Mina Martin, formerly a crime analyst at the Police Services of Winnipeg, now lovingly covered Ludwig Lacose's body with a sheet. No one should have to see him like that. No one should remember him this way.

She preferred to remember that final night of his life. The last night she'd spent with him. When he'd finally seen her. Seen her as a woman with all her love to give. All coldness melted away and the tears leaked from her eyes and down her face. She covered her mouth and screamed in silence. Some morticians had a habit of hovering. She was thankful this one— Morty, she had nicknamed him—had left her alone while she "examined the body."

Mina Martin no longer worked at the police services—far from it. But Morty didn't know that. Not yet. They'd kept Mina active and listed her as *on leave* in hopes that she would return. She no longer played for the good team. She was an outlaw, a fugitive from justice, who had chosen love only to align herself in life with a star-crossed lover.

The mission was doomed from the start. She wished she had calculated that possibility. If she could rewind time, she'd beg him not to go. Or better yet, to take her with him. She would've killed his murderer without a second glance. Then they would have ridden off into the sunset to live happily ever after, or some other cliché that didn't leave her lover dead at the end of the story.

Before she covered the face of her beloved, she leaned over and kissed his rigid blue lips. She heard a noise behind her. She straightened, quickly wiped her tears, and jammed a pair of oversized sunglasses on her face.

"He's really not breathing," she tried to joke lightly as they sometimes did in this business. Had they seen her kiss him? Her pulse sped at the thought. She turned slowly with a sad half-smile on her face. The mortician was standing with a middle-aged blond woman, who looked like she had once been pretty. Now she carried about thirty extra pounds around her mid-section, and her face sagged a little.

Mina stifled a gasp, not only at her poor timing with her morbid joke, but at the fact that his wife now stood in the room with her. With them. His wife was the third wheel.

She doesn't belong here with us, Mina thought protectively, fighting the urge to order her out of the room.

Summoning every ounce of professionalism she possessed, Mina put her shoulders back and walked forward. She paused in front of the wife. Mina spontaneously grabbed her hand. For one moment, Mina identified acutely with the wife's pain. As she looked into her eyes, Mina knew his wife did not know about her.

"Becky, I'm so sorry for your loss," Mina said quietly.

Becky Lacose stiffly nodded. Her face was white. Her eyes kept straying just beyond Mina. To Lacose. Mina released her hand and walked out the door.

His wife and the mortician were none the wiser. Mina had no right to be there. She had no claim to that man. No position of authority that would make anyone open the door and let her in. But they did. From that realization, an idea began to form.

She got into her car and stared at nothing in front of her for minutes. Then Mina lay her head on the steering wheel, remembering the night she'd learned of his death, and cried.

Had it really been twenty-four hours since Mina Martin laid sobbing on the cold tile floor in his kitchen? She had been too weak to get up and go to bed. She had been too tired to care. She had been too heartbroken to feel the cold floor under her. She had been painfully aware she was utterly alone. Again.

One minute, she'd been looking around for a bottle of champagne to celebrate a victory and the impending return of her lover.

The next minute, Mina had been crushed by the news of his death. The news that had come as a text from a former coworker who thought Mina would celebrate the death of that *vile serial killer*, Ludwig Lacose. He—her love—was dead. Murdered. Pushed violently. He'd plummeted out of a five-story window. *Paige* had murdered him. Paige had changed everything from the day she'd started working at the police services.

Nothing could have saved him. No one, not even Mina, could have kept him alive despite her advanced tech skills, her creative problem solving, and her newly kindled love for him. He'd been on a suicide mission from the beginning. No one could have kept him safe. Least of all Mina. She understood that now. The mission was doomed to fail from the beginning. All because Paige had stepped in to ruin their lives.

Doom, doom, doom, Mina had droned on to herself while lying on that floor, her tears momentarily subsiding. She had made a small salt-water puddle on the floor next to her head. When she'd been with him, she'd had purpose. Her life had held meaning. In such a short time, he had become her everything. Now that he was dead, she wanted to die along with him.

She could die. Or she could kill his murderer. It was all her fault. That nasty little traitor had betrayed them all and changed the course of Mina's life forever. Paige Mynart had taken the one person who had been precious to Mina. Because of Paige, Mina's love was dead.

What do I do now? Mina had whimpered aloud as she looked up at the ceiling. It was his ceiling in his apartment, which was his secret lair, nestled in a forgotten corner of an apartment building.

The rest of Lacose's team was dead too. Every one of them had been killed on that mission. The darkness of night surrounded the silence that echoed in her ears.

Get up, a male voice had finally answered. The voice was as clear as the last time he'd spoken to Mina. *Finish the plan.*

Darling? Mina had sat up suddenly, her heart fluttering with hope. She'd peered into the night. She couldn't see him, but she felt his presence as if he were standing in the room with her.

You are my clever minx, and this floor is beneath you, he'd said in a strong, commanding voice.

Mina had giggled. *Of course the floor is beneath me! Who's clever now?*

Go to bed, Mina, he'd said. *You have a long day of planning ahead of you.*

I do? Mina was on her feet now. She peered into the black apartment. Though she still couldn't see him, she had obeyed him. She'd gotten up. But she hadn't gone to her own room, she'd gone to his. She lay down in his big, warm bed and remembered the last time they were together. She could almost feel his strong arms around her.

There, as she fell asleep in his bed, she knew she would move forward with a new emotion in place of sadness in order to function. Anger. Anger would be her new companion. Anger would help Mina come up with a new plan and a new purpose.

Now, sitting in her car, she lifted her head, wiped her eyes, and turned the car key in the ignition. It would be a very long time before Mina would recover from the pain and heart-wrenching grief over losing him. But she'd mourn later. Right now, she needed to focus.

After all, it was only a matter of time before someone Paige treasured fell into her petite hands. Mina would be there to scoop up the object of Paige's love and destroy him the way Paige had destroyed Mina's lover. All Mina had to do was wait for an opportunity. Or create one.

1

JAMES

Orange, red, and yellow leaves adorned the trees under a dark, overcast sky. According to my wife, Paige, in another week or two, the leaves will fall and the trees will be bare, opening up the forest surrounding our little cabin home. She also mentioned that this fall has been colder than normal.

Case in point, the cold autumn wind whipped around the yard as I watched my three-and-a-half-year-old bonus daughter, Anna, chase Molly, our lovable golden retriever. I could feel my hair, the crazy black mop of curls, blowing around on top of my head. It might be time for a haircut. I pulled my jacket tighter. I was used to the cold, having originated from Canada. After a time of intense chaos, my life had become simple, and I took great joy in that. This was my new normal.

There was a time not too long ago when complications ruled my life, and I didn't cope well. That's an understatement. I discovered I'm an addict who chooses substances to cope when life *happens*. For me life had *happened* in a big way, about two or three times, and one of those times had almost killed me.

When I was sober and managing well, I chose laughter and found it drew people to me. During my good days, I had a lot of friends and was mostly outgoing. During my bad days—well, I don't remember a lot of my bad days. Nor do I want to. Which is why I now cherish my time with my daughter, our dog, and my beautiful wife.

"Hi," Paige said, right on cue. She attempted to hug me from behind, but her arms didn't make it around me.

"I was just thinking about you!" I said warmly as I spun to put my arms around her. These days that was getting harder to do on account of her third-trimester pregnancy.

"Really? What were you thinking?" Paige lifted her face. I looked into her piercing, deep-green eyes and smoothed her long, straight brown hair as the wind blew it around her face.

"About how big you're getting," I teased with an impish smile on my face. I couldn't resist.

"Hey!" Paige hit my arm lightly, but the smile on her face told me I hadn't stepped too far over the line.

"Fine, I was thinking about how big the *babies* are getting." I put my hand on her stomach and was rewarded with a kick. I couldn't stop smiling. Pregnancy looked beautiful on my wife. She was glowing. By the time we figured out she was pregnant, she was about three months along. We only had to wait a month to find out we were having twins—one girl and one boy. I'd always wanted kids. To find out I would have one of each gender on the first attempt was miraculous. If that wasn't cool enough, they were due on Halloween.

"Please don't go to Canada," Paige requested in a quiet voice. She wrapped her arms around me, shivering in the cold. She watched as our daughter, Anna, tried to jump on Molly's back.

"Paige, we've been over this before. I have to. Gilly has a buyer for the company. These things need to move fast, or the deal will die. The sooner I sell, the sooner I can close all doors to my past and settle down with you and the kids, right here in Missouri. The timing could not be better."

"Anna, be gentle," Paige called, momentarily distracted.

Anna stopped tugging at Molly's leg and made a face. "Aww!" she protested loudly.

"Besides," I went on, "I'll be back in two days."

"I don't know, James. I have a really bad feeling about this." She lowered her voice, "And Anna is really getting to be a handful. What if I can't handle her and being pregnant at the same time by myself?" her words trailed into a whisper.

I knew her well enough to know she didn't admit weakness unless she was really afraid. I pulled her closer to me. I cupped my hand around her head and held it against my chest so she could hear my heartbeat. It always raced wildly when she was around. That was partly because we were still technically newlyweds.

I had met Paige when Anna was still a baby. I had claimed Anna as my own daughter. Her father wasn't around at the time. Paige thought he was dead. By all rights, I could have stepped in and legally adopted her once we married. It was even my plan to do so. Then Stephen, her birth father, showed up a little more alive than Paige remembered.

It turned out, Stephen was a good guy, which made it easy to coexist in a nice co-parenting unit. Most days I felt like Anna's father though, since Stephen's job took him away much of the time. I wasn't trying to replace him. I just stood in that place when he wasn't in town.

"Paige." I turned and looked her in the eyes. I paused. Those intense green eyes. I could get lost in them. "I would never discount or debate your feelings. You know that. You have more intuition in your toe than I have in my whole body—"

Paige giggled but sobered and rolled her eyes at me.

"And you have legitimate reasons to be worried," I said with a sigh. "Look, bad things do happen. They happen to everyone, not just to you or me. But the strong ones overcome. That's us. We're overcomers. We don't let the darkness of the past overwhelm us or determine our future. We let the past stay in the past and move forward."

She took a deep breath and blinked away tears that had filled her eyes but didn't quite spill. She nodded bravely.

"You've been through a lot. We both have. But look—" I pointed to Anna who was now on her back mimicking Molly. Both of them had feet and paws up in the air. It was such a normal sight, I forgot to laugh. Not to mention, this was a serious conversation. "She came back to us. Sometimes it's intuition and sometimes it's just fear."

"Yeah." Paige looked away. I knew her well enough to know she was replaying the year we spent searching for Anna when she'd been kidnapped. I knew she still blamed herself. Her gaze was far past the trees, her eyes haunted by the ghosts of the past.

Her story had started right here in this little cabin we called home, out here in the middle of nowhere, Missouri, surrounded by woods. This home had belonged to her parents until the day her dad was murdered in it and her mom had run away.

Regardless of that fact, Paige had found her way here after her mother had been murdered. To have both parents murdered was unthinkable to me. It made me admire my wife. Paige was a survivor.

Unfortunately, that wasn't the end of her story. I met her—or re-met her—in Canada. She and her mom had lived there for a short time when Paige was five, and Paige and I had been in kindergarten together. They disappeared in the night, and I barely had a chance to say *goodbye*. I didn't think I'd ever see her again.

When I saw her at a grocery store in Canada decades later, my lame *Don't I know you?* pick up line actually worked because it was true. From the moment we met, there had been a connection, an instant attraction, and a familiarity. She felt it too, which is why she'd let her guard down with me so quickly.

"It's just..." Paige's voice trailed off. Despite all Paige's positive characteristics, she had a negative one too. She was an overthinker, a worrier. It was a small price to pay. Not to mention, she had a right to be this way. "A lot went wrong in Canada the last time."

"The bad guy is dead, babe. He's gone," I whispered as I kissed the top of her head.

The *bad guy* was Ludwig Lacose. The man who had been her boss and mentor. He'd turned out to be a dirty cop who'd kidnapped our Anna and tried to kill Paige. In the end, she'd exposed his crimes, which landed Lacose behind bars. Until he broke out.

He'd sent a message straight to Paige in the form of a blood letter. He'd killed her best friend, Brittany, in Canada and left a note on Brittany's body. The note said he was coming for Paige next, and he did. Though Paige was placed in witness protection, Lacose had somehow found her in the hidden WITSEC location in Georgia. But Stephen, who had shown up to warn her about Lacose, had ended up killing Lacose, with Paige's help, in defense of their own lives. That year in WITSEC had started Paige on a course that ultimately led to years without Anna. We just got Anna back earlier this year.

"What if—" she began again. "You fall off again while you're gone?"

I tensed. I knew that was coming. It was my own fault, and I had to answer for it. She had a right to ask me.

"I don't think I will. But yeah," I could still hear the Canadian lilt in the way I pronounced words like *yeah*, and still said *eh* all the time, "it's possible."

"Do you have a plan?" she asked.

"Yeah," I answered quickly. "I did some research and plan to go to a meeting I found. That, and I'll call my sponsor every day. But remember, it's two days, Paige. What can go wrong in two days?"

I should have known better than to ask the question.

"Everything can go wrong," Paige sniffed.

"Remember what to do when you feel like this?" I asked.

She pointed upward. "Take my fears to my higher power?"

I smiled. "It's the best you can do."

"What if the answer to your protection is *no*?"

I gave an over-exaggerated shudder. "Then I guess I'll die a hideous, gruesome death, and the birds will peck my eyes out."

"Not funny," Paige grumbled.

Anna giggled at me, having run by at just the right time. She'd overheard my words.

She sang, "They'll peck your eyes out!"

"Look what you did now." Paige pulled away from me, pouting.

"Hey," I pulled her back in and dropped my face to hers. I kissed her slowly until she reluctantly kissed me back.

"Ew, gross!" Anna shouted and ran inside with Molly on her heels.

"The grossest," I murmured with a smile before I deepened the kiss. *I will never tire of kissing this woman.* But as I kissed her, a tiny seed of fear planted in my heart. *What if I get on that plane tomorrow and never kiss her again?* This time my shudder was real.

Paige broke away and looked at me with question.

"It's cold," I explained it away. "Let's go inside."

2

MINA, 25 YEARS AGO

Mina was hiding under the bed again. Her breath was shallow and shuddered. The air was stagnant under the bed and Mina had a hard time breathing. She could smell her stinky shoes from where she'd taken them off right beside the bed.

Her little four-year-old body was shaking. Her dad had come home angry again. Mina knew, even in her young mind, when dad was angry, there would be trouble. Under this bed, Mina was safe.

Mina had been in the kitchen, standing on a step stool, helping her mom make dinner when they heard the front door slam loudly. The sound of big, heavy boots had echoed through the small living room. Her mother's hands had paused over dinner. Mina froze. Mina's chocolate-brown eyes looked at her mom in question.

Chocolate-brown eyes—that's what daddy said on happy days.

"Run, Mina!" Her mom had knelt down and whispered to her. "Make yourself invisible, Mina."

Mina did as she was told. She ran through the door off the kitchen that connected to her bedroom. It wasn't the first time she'd done this. She fell flat on her tummy, ignoring the way the air whooshed out of her. She army-crawled herself under the bed.

Army crawl. That's what her daddy said the green, plastic army men did when they set them up on the floor to play with them.

But they weren't playing now. Her entire body quaked in fear. Her teeth chattered so loudly, she thought they must hear her in the kitchen. They did not.

"Chicken?" Mina could hear her dad yell. "I don't want chicken! We had that last night. Don't you know how to make anything else?"

"I'm sorry, Lawrence," her mother responded. Mina could hear how shaky her mom's voice sounded. "I can make you something else. It'll just be a little longer."

Mina heard the smack of her father's hand as it connected with her mother's skin. She cried out but covered her mouth.

"Are you mouthin' me, woman?" her dad bellowed.

"No!" her mom cried. "I just thought you might be hungry."

"I am hungry. I work all day long so you can stay home with our brat, and you can't even get dinner on the table in time for when I get home?"

"I'm sorry!" Her mom's voice trembled.

"Get it done, Mary!"

Then there was silence. Mina could hear her mom crying. At least, she thought it was her mom. Then she realized it was coming from her. She took a big gulp of air and let it out slowly in an effort to keep quiet and stop crying. She mustn't be seen or heard lest she become a target of her dad's rage.

He thinks I'm a brat, Mina sniffed. That hurt her feelings.

Be invisible, Mina. Her mom's words came back to her.

The words bounced around her heart and became her life mantra.

Be invisible, Mina. So, she was.

3

STEPHEN

Stephen Wilton combed through his blond, curly hair in frustration and made a gesture like he was about to pull it out of his head. He and three other officers were wearing black clothing with black bullet-proof vests. They had stopped a train for an unscheduled search, certain they would finally find who they'd been looking for.

The night had been a bust—one in a long string of disappointing near misses as they tracked a criminal who was more ruthless than any of them had ever seen. He'd killed his own parents in a fit of rage. He'd killed the brother of a known crime boss. He'd killed the woman Stephen had loved. He knew who Stephen's daughter was. There was talk that Stephen was *too* invested in finding him, that Stephen's motivation was *too* personal. Maybe they were right. Maybe Stephen was out for revenge.

More than that, he tried to convince himself, *I need to protect my daughter.*

He needed Demitri Abbott behind bars. Only, Demitri Abbott had eluded them all at every sting operation. Stephen marveled at this man's resourcefulness. Demitri had managed to lead multiple US Marshals on a trail that should have ended with his capture. More than once. But each time, at every location, Demitri Abbott had gotten away. It was starting to feel like Demitri was toying with them.

What baffled Stephen the most about Demitri were the rumors and interactions that reinforced the suspicion that Demitri had multiple personality disorder. They knew of three personalities, but for all they knew, there were far more. The multiple personalities certainly didn't impair Demitri's ability to escape. In fact, Stephen had to wonder if this was more of a superpower than a disadvantage. Each of Demitri's personalities seemed to work together to protect the others, enabling him to stay ahead of the police.

"How does a guy like that get away? Every single time!" Stephen raged between gritted teeth. This job was a lot harder than his previous role as detective. He'd experienced some hard cases back then. But this job wore on him. Although he had the freedom to cross state lines and follow a criminal over borders, and had done so, he found it took much more of his mental capacities to focus and stay sharp. He also found he got way less sleep than ever before.

"Well, boss?" asked a stocky man named Booker, who was Stephen's partner.

Stephen's eyes were still searching the dark horizon for movement. There was none. The air was warm, still, and stagnant. They all stood silent and motionless in the New Mexico canyon, reluctant to admit defeat again.

Stephen wasn't the boss, but they'd put him in charge because he had some experience with Demitri. At least, he'd seen the outcome of Demitri's destruction. Stephen tried not to remember that moment. He'd arrived minutes after Demitri had put a bullet in Carley's abdomen. Somehow, Demitri had eluded him that night and every other night he'd attempted to find him.

But Stephen chose to believe each sting operation brought them closer. They had Demitri on the run, he was sure of it.

"He can't run forever," Stephen said. His pride stung. His fear overpowered his pride as he made the call. "Move it out. He's not here."

Booker nodded curtly, but his face resembled Stephen's. "We'll find him. Sooner or later, he'll slip. We'll be right there when he does."

Stephen mirrored Booker's curt nod and got in his car.

He was determined to see Demitri behind bars, if it was the last thing he ever did.

4

JAMES

I grabbed my carry-on bag and stepped off the plane in
Winnipeg, Canada, the place I'd called home my whole life.
Only it wasn't my home anymore. My parents were here, and I
might call their house a second home. It was, after all, the place
where I'd spent most of my childhood.

But, as I'd explained to my parents, I was really here because
I'd gotten an offer on my business. The offer was one I could
not refuse, and it had come at the perfect time. Still, I'd had to
talk it over with my parents. It was a family business, after all.
I'd inherited the corporate construction company after my
grandfather passed away. The rift between my grandfather and
my dad had made it no surprise when I was named heir, not my
father.

To be honest, I'd had my own rift with my father growing
up, which had caused me to move in with my grandfather and
work for him far before a teenager should be doing manual
labor. But grandfather had done all the legal work to make a
fifteen-year-old "work-ready." It had something to do with
passing legal guardianship to my grandfather, which also hadn't

sat well with my dad, but he'd signed off anyway. It had made much more sense when Grandad had drawn up paperwork to pass the company to me when he'd died. By the time that went down, my older sister had already moved away with her husband and my niece and nephew.

Paige had been livid with me when I explained why I was going back to Canada.

Not only is this a great offer on the company, I'd explained, *it's the best possible timing.* It would make it that much easier for me to officially relocate my life to Missouri to be with Paige, Anna, and coming soon—the twins.

I just want to have all of this taken care of before the babies are born, I'd told her logically.

You have to be here for the birth, she'd argued. *I'm due in less than a month. What if I go into labor early? That happens, you know. Especially with twins. Can't you wait until afterwards?*

Paige, you're going to need me a lot more after the babies are here than you need me right now. Besides, this offer has a time limit. These people are only in Canada for a week, and they want to make this deal in person. Not to mention, I have to sign papers. Let me do this. For us. We'll be set after this, and I'll fly back home a much richer man.

Once off the plane, I pulled out my phone for a quick check-in. Paige answered on the first ring.

"Did you make it?" Paige asked. She sounded breathless.

"Yes, just got off the plane." I laughed at the way she bypassed any greeting. "Everything is just fine."

"I miss you so much. You better be back here before the babies are born, mister!"

"Yes, ma'am!" I tried to be serious when I said the words. I looked up just then and saw my name on a posterboard sign as I got off the escalator. "I have to go. My ride is here. I'll call you later tonight. Say *hi* to Anna for me."

"Say *hi* yourself," Paige said.

Anna must have yanked the phone away. "Hi!"

"Hi, princess. Are you taking good care of mommy?" I asked.

"No. She's grumpy!" Anna said with a pout in her voice.

I laughed aloud. "Be nice to mommy. She's got babies growing in her."

"The babies are fat!" Anna giggled.

I laughed again.

Paige got back on the phone. "I love you, James. Don't you forget it."

"Never in a million." I couldn't stop smiling.

I hung up the phone and walked up to the woman holding the sign with my name on it. Her hair was raven black, short, and choppy. It framed her thin pixie face. Her eyeliner was dark and drawn like cat-eyes. At least, that was what Paige called it when she wore her makeup like that.

"James?" asked the woman holding the sign. She was thin and petite, despite her three-inch high-heel boots. She was dressed in black and looked like a professional.

"Yes," I answered.

"I have a car waiting for you to escort you to the meeting," she informed me as she began to walk quickly out of the airport. I followed her, feeling pleased not to have to hail a cab.

"Fancy," I smiled. "They didn't tell me they were sending a car."

"Only the best," she responded lightly. "I'm your new administrative assistant, by the way."

"I didn't know I had a new assistant," I said as I got into a nice black Cadillac SUV with tinted windows.

"I'm Mina Martin." She climbed into the back seat of the car and sat next to me. There was a man with dark blond hair in the driver's seat.

As I turned to close the door to the car, I didn't see the syringe full of clear fluid in Mina's hand, nor did I have time to react when she injected it into the vein in my neck. I didn't even have time to respond as I blacked out in the back of the moving vehicle, unaware that the direction we traveled was not the direction of an acquisitions meeting, but a direction far away from it.

5

PAIGE

"Come on, Anna. We'll be late to karate," Paige told her daughter as she searched for her car keys.

"I don't wanna go," Anna informed her.

"Oh, Anna, we've been through this. Your daddy thinks karate is important for you. He wants you to learn how to be a real ninja and make new friends. It's not optional." Paige didn't tell Anna she agreed with Stephen.

"What's optional mean?" Anna asked.

"It means you don't have a choice." Paige stopped looking and glanced at Anna suspiciously. "Have you seen mommy's keys, Anna?"

Anna shook her head from side to side slowly. "No-o," she sang, letting the second "o" lilt upward. It was her tell. Paige knew when Anna was lying because she started sing-songing her words with extra syllables.

"Anna, did you hide mommy's keys?" Paige tried again, her frustration rising a notch.

"No-o," Anna sang again.

Paige sighed and walked into Anna's room. She surveyed the messy bedroom, remembering the time when Anna was missing and Paige had cleaned the room, put her toys in a memory box, and upgraded the bed to a "big girl" bed. It hadn't stayed clean for long. Anna was a messy child. Which is why it was going to be hard to find those keys.

Paige began by moving toys into a neat, organized pile and surveying the carpet. She sank to her knees, knowing it would be hard to get back up on account of the two babies growing inside her. She pulled everything out from underneath Anna's bed with a grunt. She made a second pile. No car keys.

Out of breath, Paige sat back, her bottom on the floor and her legs out in front of her. Anna peeked in the doorway of her room, looking sheepish. She held her hand behind her back.

"I'm sorry, mommy," Anna said as she took a tentative step into the room.

"Why are you sorry, Anna?" Paige asked.

"Promise not to be mad?" Anna asked, taking another step forward.

"Oh, Anna." Paige felt tired and resigned. If only Anna knew the real reason they wanted her in karate. Paige thought about the phone call she'd gotten from Stephen a few weeks after Anna came home.

We lost him again, Paige. Every time we get close, Demitri Abbott slips right by us. We've been chasing him all this time. We just don't have any more leads.

What does this mean for us? What should we do here? Paige had asked him.

We need to prepare ourselves in case he shows up. He knows Anna. I don't have any reason to think he'd come after her. But he seems to be taunting us. Like he's having a good time messing with us. We're all baffled about how he's doing this.

Prepared how, Stephen? Paige had asked in a different way. Her eyes had fallen on Anna, who had been lying on the floor watching TV.

We need to teach her self-defense, he'd stated.

23

Stephen, she's three! Paige had protested, feeling shocked.

Three and a half but acts like she's five already, he'd retorted. *How about karate? They have classes for little kids, don't they? She always wanted to be a ninja. Tell her she can now. I don't care how we do it. We just need to get her enrolled. Until Demitri is put away, don't assume she's safe.*

Paige had hung up the phone, feeling unsettled. She'd enrolled Anna that day. Only, Anna didn't seem to want to be a ninja anymore. Paige thought she might have outgrown it.

Now, Anna quietly walked forward and put a tiny fist in front of Paige's face. She opened her fist to reveal Paige's car keys.

"Oh, Anna. Come here." Paige held out her hands and Anna snuggled around Paige's large abdomen and on her lap. "Why don't you want to go to karate?"

"I dunno," Anna said. Her face was against Paige's shirt and her voice was muffled, making it hard to hear.

"Your daddy wants you to take karate," Paige repeated. "He says it's important."

"Why?" Anna whined. "Karate is boring."

"I'm sorry you feel that way," Paige said. "He thought it would help you be a ninja."

"I don't wanna be a ninja!" Anna was suddenly angry. She sat up and glared at Paige.

"Okay." Paige put her palms up. "Why don't you want to be a ninja?"

"Because Mama Carley died," Anna whispered. Tears welled in her eyes.

"Oh, Anna!" Paige forgot to be annoyed at the way Anna called her kidnapper 'mama.' "What does that have to do with being a ninja? That wasn't your fault!"

"A ninja could have saved her," Anna said.

"No." Paige reached out and rubbed Anna's arm. "A ninja can only save herself. But she needs to know how."

"Really?" Anna asked. She sounded suspicious.

"Really. It wasn't your job to save her, Anna. What happened was terrible. But it wasn't your fault. You did good. Staying quiet was exactly what you were supposed to do. It was the only thing you could do."

Anna was quiet as she thought this through.

Paige rolled to her knees and worked to get up off the floor. "Let's go before we're late."

As Paige drove Anna to karate, she marveled that she'd just had such a mature conversation with her daughter at such a young age. Not for the first time, Paige wondered if school screenings would reveal just how advanced Anna was for her age when she got to kindergarten. In the meantime, Anna had taken several psychological tests and Paige had accepted that her daughter's logic surpassed her age.

When they arrived, she watched as Anna bowed at the door and greeted her sensei. Paige certainly had no idea if karate would help Anna defend herself one day, but she thought it would at least teach Anna respect for her elders.

6

MINA, 12 YEARS AGO

Mina checked her watch before she walked through the door. She exhaled the breath she had been holding and watched it form a cloud of warmth in the frozen night air. Alaska was a sort of frozen hell in the winter. Not to mention the forever darkness that plagued these months. Mina hated Alaska. But not as much as she hated this house.

The house itself was fine. It was a sturdy little warm brick home. She could see smoke releasing into the air from the chimney at the top of the practical black roof. She walked slowly up the slippery stairs. Everything froze immediately in this weather, and it had snowed a stint earlier in the day.

Mina paused to turn up the music she was listening to on her iPod shuffle and adjust where it was clipped onto her jacket. She'd bought it with the money she'd made from her fast-food job. The technology in Alaska was behind the States, she'd heard. But she was happy to have music in any form it came.

Though she was convinced her dad would be passed out for the night, she quietly opened the front door. It was her thing. If she could slide through the door at the right time, she'd go unnoticed.

Invisible.

Tonight, her plan didn't work.

"Mina!" her mom's voice snapped at her. "Where have you been? It's after midnight, I was worried sick about you! It's a school night."

Mina didn't try to cover her annoyance over her mom's loud voice. She was going to wake him.

"Don't be. I work every night. Are you just now noticing?" Mina followed her sarcastic reply with a smirk. She'd gotten off work hours ago but had gone to a friend's house to hang out. Anything to avoid going home.

He came out of nowhere. She didn't even suspect he'd still be up. But he was. The hit to her head landed with such power, she found herself lying on the floor in pain, wondering what had just happened.

She didn't have to wonder long. He kicked her hard in the stomach. The air whooshed out of Mina's body fast, replaced by sharp pain.

"Don't you ever talk to your mother like that again!" Her dad's angry voice made its way through the pain that temporarily clouded her hearing. "We called work. We know you weren't there. You off whoring around?"

"That's enough," her mother ordered sharply.

"Shut up!" he responded. Mina heard a smack she assumed landed on her mother, but that was nothing new. He kicked her mom around all the time. But until today, he hadn't ever touched Mina.

Mina felt her eyes overflow with involuntary tears. How had she planned that so wrong? She was so good at getting in and out of the house unseen. Now, she was on his radar.

Run away, Mina! Don't ever come back, her brain urged her. There was a problem though. Mina couldn't seem to get off the floor. She caught sight of her mom weeping as she lay in a crumpled heap not far from her. Her dad had stormed off.

Why can't I move? Mina wondered. She closed her eyes, welcoming the darkness as a break from the pain she was in. She lay in that darkness for what felt like days. She would find out later that her mom had finally gotten the courage to take Mina to the hospital around two that morning. She'd gone next door to get a neighbor to help her lift Mina into the car after her dad had passed out. By then, Mina had already slipped into a coma on account of the concussion she'd received.

When she finally woke up, Mina discovered she had two broken ribs from the kick. She was alone. Her mom had no doubt rushed back home before her husband could wake and catch her helping Mina. When doctors had asked Mina what happened, she'd told them she'd been in a fight. She didn't tell them who with.

The hospital released her to a distant cousin Mina had only met once or twice. Her mom must have signed paperwork giving authorization so she could leave the hospital with them. Mina didn't go back home. Not immediately, anyway. Her older cousin allowed her to stay as long as Mina promised never to go back home where her dad was. It seemed her dad had caused a rift in the family. It was in that home that Mina had met her cousin's son, who had been worse than her father in some ways. She had to leave there as well. Not only did Mina lack the courage to stay and fight him, she knew she would not win.

After she'd run away from her cousin's house and her rapist son, she found she had burned her bridge with the only family she'd had left. When there was no more family left, she'd found friends who let her crash on their couches. It was years before she went back home, and when she did, it was only because her mom was in danger. In the meantime, she'd worked her way through high school and finished at eighteen.

Mina learned she was freakishly smart, but she hadn't known because her attention had been so divided with all the drama at home. With her dad out of the picture, Mina excelled. The more accolades she got from teachers, the better she did. Positive attention from authority figures was a bigger high to her than any drink or drug she'd ever tried. All Mina had to do was be excellent, perfect, and unseen. How hard would that be?

7

JAMES

I woke up with a gasp and sat up with a jerk. The room was pitch black. For one sinking second, it was the same sensation as waking up after falling off the wagon. I had no idea where I was. My head hurt. I put my hand up to my neck and felt an isolated tender spot. I couldn't remember what had happened.

I could feel a soft mattress under me. I was lying on a smooth, nicely made bed. I took inventory of my physical body. My hands and arms were free. My feet were unbound, my shoes were still on my feet. I swung them over the edge of the bed. My feet hit the floor.

I stood and put my hands out in front of me. I couldn't see. Either my eyes weren't adjusting to the dark room, or the walls were all black. I thought it was probably the latter, though I didn't know why anyone would paint a room black. I walked until I felt a wall. Then, I felt along the side of the wall until I found a light switch.

I flipped the switch and blinked heavily as unexpectedly bright light flooded the room. There was a door right in front of me. I tried the doorknob. No luck. The doorknob didn't even turn. I inspected the door further but found no lock. The lock must be on the other side of the door.

"Hello?" I cleared my throat. Could anyone hear me? I looked around the room, taking inventory. I had, indeed, been laying on a soft bed. The bed took up most of the room. I guessed it was a queen bed, and the room was small. The floor under my feet had a firm, low-quality carpet on it. There was another door that was propped open slightly. I edged my way closer and saw that it was a bathroom, complete with a shower. I opened a pantry door and discovered towels. But there was no way out of this room.

"Oh, good. You're up," a female voice addressed me through some intercom system. Her voice sounded monotonous and a little robotic.

I whirled around. I slowly walked out of the bathroom. I spotted an intercom speaker in the upper corner of the room.

"Does this help?" the voice asked.

I heard the sound of a low motor whirring as dark blinds appeared to roll up into the wall, leaving a window of sight between the room where I stood and the rest of the place. Wherever this place was.

I immediately looked through the glass to see what resembled a small IT command center out in the main room. It looked like a computer room with a few pieces of furniture pushed up against the walls.

There was a small woman standing on the other side of the glass in the next room, which looked more like a business center than a living room. She was petite, even while wearing black boots with a three-inch heel. She had short black hair that flipped around her face. Her eyes sparkled and were lined with black eyeliner. She wore black jeans and a black top. She was the woman from the airport. *My assistant*, she had said.

I put my hands out to touch the glass partition between us.

"No, no, I wouldn't do that if I were you." The woman's

tone did not invite discussion. "It's plexiglass, but it's not going anywhere."

"What do you want from me?" I asked. I was truly baffled about why someone would go to so much trouble. "Do I owe you money or have unfinished business with you?"

"James, it's me, Mina." She walked closer to the window and peered in with her hands on her hips.

Her eyes were narrowed and there was a look of disappointment on her face. She might have been pretty if she just smiled.

"I'm sorry." I shook my head. She was unfamiliar to me. "Did we meet when I was drinking? I had a problem in the past—"

"No. Focus, James. We never met, but I assumed Paige at least mentioned me from her days of working at the Police Service of Winnipeg?" Mina asked.

"I'm sorry," I scratched my head. "I just don't remember. But perhaps we could get Paige on the phone to be a part of this little reunion?" I smiled my most charming smile.

"Nice try." Mina's expression settled into irritation. Her eyes, which resembled a cat's, looked spiteful. She appeared to be mad and walked away, muttering, "Trust Paige to ruin my plan."

"Oh, good," I tried again to win her over. "I love a good plan. Care to share?"

Mina whipped back around. She crossed her arms and studied me for half a minute. "Okayyy," she drew out the word like she was deciding where to start. She walked to a wall that held a very large whiteboard. She tapped on it.

"That looks complicated," I said with a shrug. "Can you explain?"

Mina took a few steps back toward me. "It's really quite simple, James. It's just written in code. Let me decipher it for you," she snapped.

"Please," I encouraged her, trying to act like being locked in

a room by a demented woman was an everyday occurrence
for me.

"Step one, lure you to a fake business meeting in order to
kidnap you."

"Oh no!" I interrupted with a groan. "The meeting was fake?
No one is buying my business?"

"Oh, the meeting was very real," Mina corrected. "I'm the
one who set it all up. On both sides. It was brilliant, really."

"So, there were women and men at that business meeting?
And we were going to talk about the sale of my business. But I
didn't show up?" I felt a deep sense of dread in my stomach.
Who was this woman to muck about in my life?

"Correct. It's only a matter of time before it's obvious you
are missing instead of just a no show." Her fingers made air
quotes when she spoke the words *no show*.

"So, I go missing, then what happens?" I pointed at the
board.

"Your wife comes looking for you." Mina pointed to a string
of jargon on the whiteboard that I didn't understand.

"Great. Does she find me?" I asked, feeling both denial
about the danger I was in and hopeful this was all just some
silly game.

"Yes! That's the best part of the plan." Mina clapped her
hands together.

"Well, this sounds very easy so far." I clasped my hands
together. I put on a show of being impressed and entertained by
this crazy woman's idea but inside, I was panicking. To me, this
woman came off insane. *Why would anyone go to all this trouble?*
Paige couldn't get on a plane at over eight months pregnant.
Worse, she might try if she thought she needed to rescue me.

Paige! My anxiety doubled thinking about her. It wouldn't
take very long for Paige to start worrying about where I was.
Paige didn't need any stress this late in the pregnancy. I hated
that her intuition had been right all along. She hadn't wanted

me to go and now I knew why. She always did have a sixth sense.

Note to self, I mentally chastised myself, *the next time your wife has a bad feeling about something, listen to her!*

"No!" Mina said. She came right up to the window so close that I could see an intense gleam in her eye. I took a step back. "That's when things get hard for you. See, you're going to die, James. I'm going to kill you in front of Paige. I'm going to let her wallow in her sadness for a few days before I kill her too."

"No! Why would you do that? What has my poor Paige done to you?" I took several more steps back when Mina pressed her hands up against the window and stood peering in at me with a nervous intensity. She looked like she was studying a science experiment.

"She killed my love. She never should have lived to begin with. He should have killed her and come back to me. Only—" Mina's hand hit the plexiglass hard with each word to punctuate her pain. "He. Never. Came. Back."

"Oh no!" I said, puzzling out her words. I had a sinking feeling who she was talking about.

She was referring to the time after Paige and I had met years ago. Back then, Paige had lived in Canada and worked for the Police Service of Winnipeg. It was when she had discovered the Deliver and Dash Killer and they had arrested him for multiple counts of murder. He'd confessed to the murders, which had made him a serial killer. He never should have gotten back out of prison. Only, a guard had walked him right out. Paige had to go into witness protection at that point. My heart sank. This is exactly what Paige had been afraid of. I'd walked right into a trap.

"Paige doesn't deserve to live," Mina spat. Droplets from her mouth hit the window.

"Why not?" I asked, aware my voice sounded whiny.

"She was a rat!" Mina snapped. "Enough story time." She

rolled the blind back down between what appeared to be two sheets of plexiglass in the wall. Innovative. I had never seen anything like it. I crept forward wanting to study this design.

"Now what?" I asked loudly, assuming she could still hear me. I looked around my room uncertainly. I didn't feel tired. In fact, knowing her plan included my murder made me not want to sleep at all.

"We wait. It's only a matter of time before your disappearance is all over the news."

"Can I ask you a question?" I asked.

Mina made a noise I thought meant she was okay with it.

"Have you ever killed anyone before?"

Mina was quiet for a tick. "I'm not as innocent as I might look."

"Is that a *no*, then?" I felt hopeful. She didn't look like a killer. "It's just you seem like a decent person under all that anger and grief. I would hate to see you throw your life away like this—"

"Yes, James, I've killed before. Okay?" Mina snapped.

"Okay, sorry I made an assumption."

"I wasn't asking your opinion, James. I'm shutting down the com system. Try to get some sleep. You've got some seriously stressful days ahead of you."

Sudden darkness consumed the room. Clearly, she had the controls to power lights on and off. I put my hand out and found the wall. Letting my fingers trail against the wall for guidance, I found the bathroom door again.

My hand groped for the light switch. I flipped it on. When light illuminated the darkness, I felt tears cloud my vision. I flipped it on and off a few more times. I felt grateful for this one thing I could control—light.

Especially as I turned to survey the room again. The walls were, indeed, painted black. There were no pictures or paintings. Just black walls. The only furniture in the room was the bed. It was on a low bed frame. The matching black comforter tidily lay on the bed and the edges swept the floor.

I turned to look over the bathroom again but noticed the mirror was missing. The bathroom held every amenity I would need. Toilet paper, toothbrush and toothpaste, travel-sized soap, and shampoo. There were towels in the pantry. But there was no mirror.

As I flipped off the light switch and left the room, I wondered if the reason the mirror was missing was to protect Mina from me or to protect me from myself. That last thought left me feeling chilled.

8

MINA, 10 YEARS AGO

Even in the summer, the Alaskan air held a chill. Air conditioning was not needed. For the moment, they were in a good spot. Come winter, heat might be a luxury she and her new roommates could not afford. Her roommates, along with Mina, were just thankful to have a place to stay. It wasn't the nicest place, but the places where Mina had stayed in the past weren't nice either, and not one of them had a dime to spare to upgrade to anything better.

Mina was working and paying a small portion of the bill just to have a bed of her own in a small bedroom, which she shared with another girl. But Mina didn't mind. It was better than the homeless shelter.

There were four people in that trailer with two bedrooms. In the beginning, they weren't friends. They didn't talk or hangout. They just came home long enough to take a shower, change clothes, and sleep for the night. They were survivors.

In those days, work in Alaska was tight. Most job openings consisted of fast-food restaurants. Mina wasn't above working those, but she found they didn't pay enough for her to maintain her meager living. The friends she had been living with when she graduated high school had decided to get married, and Mina felt she was a third wheel. That, along with an inability to give the couple much rent money, drove her to the streets. Hotels were too expensive, and she didn't have any other friends or family she trusted.

She'd met her roommates at a homeless shelter she'd found one night when she'd finally decided it was too cold to stay another night outside. As Mina started up the steps to the shelter, a large man had assaulted her. Mina must have screamed in surprise before the hit had knocked her out. She had no recollection of what happened until she came to.

She was lying on a cot and awoke to three concerned faces she'd never seen before. At first, she sat up and tried to scramble away from them. Until one of them, the guy named Jess, put his hand on her shoulder and told her what had happened. A girl inside the shelter had heard Mina scream. She'd grabbed the nearest two people she could find. The three of them had found the man dragging Mina behind the shelter. Jess had shoved the man down from behind and roughed up his face a couple times. The two girls had grabbed Mina and carried her inside. Mina had never felt more grateful or indebted to perfect strangers in her life.

The four of them bonded quickly and had determined even more quickly that the homeless shelter was worse than the streets. The dirty, drafty warehouse building was packed with more people than they had food to go around, and the place smelled of body odor and human waste. After a week of seeing each other there and sleeping in the same corner, they'd made a plan. Between them, they could scrape together enough money waitressing, flipping burgers, or packing groceries—whatever work they chose, to afford this small trailer with two bedrooms Jess had found. No background checks needed.

Her roommates had saved her. They were all around the same age. Through no fault of their own, they had all found themselves homeless. They needed each other. That's what had bonded them together. Despite that, Mina didn't plan to let her guard down or let anyone get close to her—not even her room-mates. She couldn't afford to trust anyone.

That all changed the night her roommate had come home beat up. The girl who'd saved her now needed to be saved. Her eyelid was swollen shut and an ugly purple bruise marred the side of her face.

Mina took one look at her roommate and found a few ice cubes in the freezer. She put them in the only clean washcloth she could find and came back to put it on the girl's face. This girl was a few years younger than Mina, and since they were all still teenagers, a few years seemed like a lot.

The girl winced but complied. Mina refused to remember her name. She just called her *girl,* so she didn't get too close. Then she heard the girl crying.

Mina sat down on the floor beside the girl's bed.

"You ever been hit?" asked the girl.

"Yeah. Of course." Mina adjusted the ice to a new spot.

The girl winced again. "Someone you love?"

"Yeah. My dad. Put me in the hospital once. Nearly killed my mom more than once."

"I hope he rots in hell someday," the girl said through clenched teeth.

"Me too," Mina agreed. "Who did this?"

"My ex-boyfriend. He keeps finding me."

"Does he know where you are right now?" Mina asked, feeling alarmed.

"Not yet," the girl answered. "But he will."

After that night, she started calling the girl *sis.* They had a bond few people shared. Because few people were brave enough to admit they got hit from time to time. Both girls believed everyone got hit from time to time because they didn't know any better.

They'd been there about a month when Jess brought home a shotgun.

Mina's eyes had grown round at the sight. She didn't know these people that well. Maybe she'd made a mistake throwing in with them. Before she could bolt, Jess' words stopped her.

"We need to keep each other safe. Have each other's back. Has anyone ever shot one of these?"

No one had.

For the next few months, Jess took turns with each of them, teaching them how to shoot. According to Jess, Mina was a natural. When they were done, the shotgun sat on a hook in the living room. They had made an oath. If there was ever a break-in, or someone feared one, the nearest person would take the gun and defend the castle. Or tiny trailer, as was the case here.

No one ever needed to use the gun. Until the night Mina got that fateful call. Mina's phone rang at two in the morning. Even after Mina's brain alerted her that the noise was her cell phone and she shook the brain fog away, it still took a minute for Mina to find her phone.

"Hello?" she finally answered.

There was silence on the other end.

"Hello?" Mina pulled the phone away from her ear and looked at the screen. It was her mom.

"Are you on the phone?" her dad's angry voice yelled in the background.

"Min—"

The phone hung up abruptly.

Mina was wide awake now. She pulled on her pants, trying to be quiet.

"Where're you going?" came a quiet, sleepy voice through the darkness.

"Home, Sis. I need to check on my mom," Mina whispered. "Go back to bed." Sharing a room with this girl was the closest she'd ever come to having a sister. Mina knew she'd defend the girl like her own family if she needed to. It was the agreement in that tiny place. They were her people, and they would stick together.

"Mina? Take the gun," Sis whispered back.

Mina froze for a second as she considered the call she'd just gotten. She'd seen her mom in bad shape before. She'd watched her mom take it night after night. How long before her mother didn't live through it?

Mina finished buttoning her jeans, slipped her feet in a pair of fuzzy boots, and threw on a jacket. She grabbed her car keys, wallet, and phone.

"I mean it, Mina," Sis insisted. "Take the gun."

Mina ignored her and went out the door. Once the night air hit her, Mina felt fear. What if she went there and he did the same thing to Mina? How would she get her mom away from him? Mina turned and went back into the trailer, grabbed the gun, and threw it in the back seat of the car. She covered it with a jacket. She wasn't sure if traveling with a loaded gun was legal. She didn't know anything about gun laws. Right now, she didn't care.

When Mina arrived at her parent's house, she grabbed the key from under the front door mat. Once inside, she found her mom crumpled in a heap on the floor in the kitchen. Her mom was shaking from head to toe. She could see the blood on the floor before she got to her mom. Mina's eyes scanned the room, looking for *him*.

Mina gently put a hand on her mom's shoulder. Her mom cried out. Mina could see her mom's face was bruised and her lip was bleeding. But the biggest concern was her mom's head. There was a misshapen knot on the top of her head.

Mina hesitated. Should she move her? She felt for her phone. She didn't find it. She must have left it in the car. She should call an ambulance. She turned and ran quickly out the door to her beat up Chevy Nova.

That's when she saw him. He was leaning against the driver side door of her car. Mina stopped short and gasped.

"Surprised to see me?" her dad slurred, a jeering smile on his face. She took in his torn-up jeans with oil stains on them and the Van Halen t-shirt he was wearing.

Something in Mina snapped. All the hatred and pent-up anger she'd held on to over the years hit her all at once. She ran at him and slammed into his chest with all her force. His body was like a rock—he was average height but stocky. It felt like she'd hit a solid wall. He didn't budge. Pain surged through Mina's shoulder.

Her dad looked surprised but turned instantly angry. He shoved Mina, knocking her off balance. She took several steps back, fighting to stay upright.

"You got something to say to me, little girl?" he said through clenched teeth.

"What is wrong with you?" Mina flew at him again, her body slamming into his broad, ungiving chest.

This time, her dad hit her across the face.

Mina flew sideways but ignored the pain. "Leave me alone. Mom is practically dead in there because of you. You sick bastard! I need to call an ambulance."

"Oh no you don't," he snarled. "She got what she had coming to her."

Mina had heard those words before. She couldn't shake the feeling that time was running out. Her mom could be dying. It was his fault. He didn't care if he killed her. Mina would be next. It was time to break the cycle.

Mina ran around to the other side of the car, opened the passenger side door, and grabbed her cell phone. Then she opened the back door and slid the shot gun out of the back seat.

She turned to find her dad right behind her. She knew her dad would never let her live after this. She pointed the shot gun right at him. The gun was within his reach. Her dad swiped for it, barely missing.

Mina pulled the trigger. The sound was deafening. The effect was immediate. She could see his t-shirt darken with a ring of blood that seeped and grew to the point of saturation. The material was barely covering the now gaping hole in his chest that had immediately filled with blood. Her dad staggered backward, a look of pain and shock on his face. He fell back onto the front lawn.

Mina watched him, feeling no remorse. He closed his eyes. He gasped for breath. There was a terrible, desperate gurgle. Then his body went still. Mina crept toward him slowly, the gun still lowered in his direction.

When she got close enough, she kicked him in the side. He didn't move. She knew better than to think this wasn't a trick. Men like him didn't die, they lived forever. They were too mean and too stubborn to die. He was faking.

She stood a distance back, staring at him for at least five minutes before she chanced to creep up close enough to feel his pulse.

There was nothing.

She tried again. Maybe she was putting her finger in the wrong place? She grabbed his wrist and tried to feel a pulse. Then the realization hit. He was dead. Shock and sudden remorse filled her as she realized what she had done. She dropped the gun like it had burned her.

Mina ran back up the stairs to the house. Her mom was still lying on the floor. Her eyes were open, but her breathing was shallow.

"Mom!" Mina cried. "Stay with me." She pulled out her phone, and with trembling fingers, she dialed 911.

"Nine-one-one, what's your emergency?" the voice asked.

"My mom—she needs an ambulance." Mina rattled off the address. Without thinking, she hung up the phone.

"Did you kill him?" her mom asked in a weak voice.

"What?" Mina asked. Panic set in. *Yes. She did kill him! The gun. The gun was laying on the lawn. The ambulance would come, and they would find the gun.*

"You killed him." A tear leaked out of the corner of her mom's eye and fell on the floor.

"Are you really lying here so beat up you might not make it, and you're asking about *him*? That jackass who was going to kill you someday?" Mina was incredulous.

"Mina, is he alive?" she asked again.

"Unbelievable!" Mina exploded. "The ambulance is on the way. I'll come check on you later."

Mina stalked out the door. She picked up the gun, put it in the back seat, and threw the blanket over the top of it. Then she drove back to the trailer, walked in, and hung the shotgun on the wall.

Mina gathered the few belongings she had—what she could see of them in the dark.

"Did you kill him, Mina?" a sleepy voice whispered through the darkness.

"Go back to bed, Sis." Mina's arms were full, and she decided that was all the belongings she needed. She was irked that the girl had made that assumption. Mostly, she was irked because the assumption was correct. Only, her mom and her dad might both be dead now.

"I'm glad," she said.

"I didn't answer you, Sis. Are you going to rat me out?" Mina asked. Her reply was short and sharp. She was reacting out of fear and panic.

"No way. Never!" The girl propped herself up on her elbow.

"I have to go now. Please take care of the others." Mina turned to leave.

"Please, don't leave me," Sis suddenly sounded alert.

Mina hesitated. "I don't have time, Sis. I have to go now."

The girl jumped up. "I have to go with you. He'll find me soon if I don't."

"Hurry up," Mina hissed back.

The girl didn't have many belongings either. She turned on a light, threw on her clothes, and gathered what was left. On their way out, they stopped in the bathroom and grabbed shampoo, a hairbrush, and some makeup.

Then they got in the car. They drove for hours.

"Where are we going, Mina?" Sis finally asked, stifling a yawn.

"Winnipeg sounds nice," Mina said softly.

9

PAIGE

Paige could hear screaming. She gasped awake. She squinted her eyes in the dark. They felt salty and crusted. Then she remembered she had cried herself to sleep. James never called her last night. He didn't respond to her text messages. She had heard nothing after he'd gotten off the plane.

Paige could surmise that the meeting went well and they all went out to dinner afterwards. But it didn't explain why there was no call after he checked into his hotel room for the night. With a heavy heart that sank into her stomach, Paige remembered that Winnipeg was the place where James had last been at his worst. *Maybe he had drinking buddies there who he'd reconnected with...* No, she stopped her train of thought. She would not let herself assume the worst. James said he had a plan, and she wanted to believe him.

Now, as she peered into the darkness, she realized the person who was screaming was Anna. Paige got up when she heard the second scream and ran to Anna's room. Like every other night since Anna had come home, she was inconsolable, having re-lived her nightly terror. The dream was always the same. Anna was hiding in the closet and she could see a bad man. The man took out a gun and shot her Mama Carley, as Anna called her.

After the first dream, Paige had to control her temper when she'd heard her daughter call her kidnapper "Mama Carley." Carley had stolen Anna from Paige and kept Anna for over a year. Carley would have gotten away with it had she not been dating a man who ended up killing her in the end.

Unfortunately, Anna had seen the whole thing. At first, they didn't know for sure if Anna had seen it happen. Her father, Stephen, had rescued her from the armoire where she'd stayed hidden. They had hoped, even if Anna had seen it happen, she wouldn't remember the terrifying scene as she grew up. They hoped Anna would be able to move past her fear of night.

Then, Paige had gotten a stern lecture from the childhood counselor where they were taking Anna. Anna loved going to play with Ms. Melissa. Anna thought counseling was fun. But when Anna went out to meet her dad in the lobby, Ms. Melissa had gotten very stern with Paige.

As she explained Anna's emotions while she was playing, Ms. Melissa had mentioned "Mama Carley."

Paige had exploded.

Ms. Melissa leveled Paige with her eyes. "Have a seat, Paige."

Paige had sat.

"Carley was just as much Anna's mother during that time period as you are now. You may not agree with it. You might not like it. But you need to be patient and kindly look at things from Anna's perspective. Anna suffered a terrible trauma and it's going to take some time to get past it."

Now, in the dark of her room, Anna clung to Paige's neck, crying inconsolably. "Look in the closet," she cried.

Paige hugged her back, unsure of whether to untangle Anna's arms from her neck at that moment to go oblige her request or stay right here with her daughter.

"Look in the closet!" Anna screamed with true horror. She was now sobbing.

"Okay, Anna. Calm down," Paige said. It was getting harder to sit down on the floor, then get back up again with her bulging pregnant belly. Paige managed to get up and reached for the door.

"Noooo!" screamed Anna.

Paige hesitated. She had no idea what to do. First, Anna wanted her to look in the closet, then Anna was terrified of what would happen if Paige opened the closet doors. James would know what to do. But James wasn't here. Paige threw open the doors to the closet.

Anna got very still and quiet.

"There's nothing there, sweet girl," Paige said quietly.

Anna nodded and looked exhausted. She fell back in her bed and breathed a shuddered sigh.

"Tell you what? Why don't you come sleep in my bed for the rest of the night?" Paige offered. She'd read a lot about the importance of training children to sleep in their own beds at night. At this moment, Paige didn't care. She just knew Anna was exhausted, and Paige thought Anna needed a place to sleep tonight where she felt safe and comfortable.

As Paige tucked Anna into her bed, then climbed in to cuddle up to her, Paige knew she needed Anna too. Tonight, they needed each other to feel safe as they both battled their fears. They just needed to make it to morning.

Tomorrow, Paige would start looking for James.

10

MINA

"Good morning, Mr. Vance," Mina greeted as she passed her impeccably dressed boss. Cup of coffee in hand, Mina walked smartly to her desk. She liked the way her black three-inch heels tapped on the floor as she walked. She sounded powerful and important. It was an added bonus that the heels made her almost average height.

As she settled in at her desk, Mina had to admit she also liked this job. What started out as a ploy to gain access to James Friesen became part of a daily routine she enjoyed. True, secretarial work was mind-numbing compared to crime analysis. But Mina found she liked the change of pace. It had given her time to think and strategize.

James Friesen had turned out to be the owner of a very large construction company that not only built residential homes but had opened a corporate construction division in the past year. He had been easier to find than Mina had thought he'd be.

Until she got the job, of course. She'd learned that James never came to work anymore. In fact, he hadn't set a foot in his own building for over six months. What kind of a business owner never showed up to work? The same kind of business owner who would no-show a professional business meeting? She could hear the voice of the man she'd loved.

Clever little minx, he whispered into her ear.

Gilly Vance, the CEO, stopped at Mina's desk. Instead of saying *good morning* and walking on by, as was his daily routine, Gilly was hovering.

"Is there something I can do for you, Mr. Vance?" Mina asked. She knew her face modeled the confusion she pretended to feel. Then she pretended to remember to ask. "Oh yeah, how did the meeting go yesterday? Thanks for letting me off to go to the dentist, by the way."

"You're welcome," Gilly said, looking deep in thought. "The meeting didn't happen."

"Oh no!" Mina looked horrified. "Did I forget to print something you needed before I left?"

"No, no. You went above and beyond as usual. It's just that—"

"What?" Mina laughed. "The suspense is killing me."

"James Friesen never showed up." Gilly crossed his hands over his chest.

"What?" Mina made her voice sound confused. "He confirmed via phone call and meeting request that he would be—"

"It's not your fault, Mina," Gilly said. "Between you and me, James tends to *not show up*. I mean when he is here, it's clear he doesn't want to be. But he's been missing in action for the past year. I was surprised when he agreed to go to the meeting. But I wasn't surprised when he didn't show up for it."

"Really?" Now Mina wasn't pretending. The confusion was real and the annoyance was evident in her voice.

Gilly leaned forward and dropped his voice. "Between you and me, James has a bit of a substance abuse problem. He just got out of rehab earlier this year. I was just hoping he'd recovered for good this time."

Mina's heart sank. "This time?"

Gilly nodded. "Yeah, it's an ongoing problem."

"I see," Mina said sourly.

"Well, it's not your problem or mine, so let's just move ahead and cross our fingers that he shows for the next acquisitions meeting." Gilly held up crossed fingers and walked into his office.

Why had no one ever told Mina that before? She had known James was spending a lot of time in a bar when she was working with Lacose, but so what? Plenty of people frequented bars. It didn't mean they had substance abuse problems.

As the day went on, Mina's mood went downhill. Other than this brief acknowledgement that James no-showed the meeting, no one seemed to care. It was business as usual. Mina's plan would only work if someone noticed he was actually missing. Sooner, rather than later. She needed Paige to panic and get on a plane to Winnipeg.

At lunch time, Mina ran back to the apartment with a burger and fries. Mina parked her car in the parking garage on the lower level, thankful for the parking spot she owned right outside the tiny little apartment. This was the only apartment off the lower level of the garage. It was so tucked out of the way, Mina assumed it had been built as an on-sight maintenance worker's apartment. The apartment door looked like it would lead to a supply closet. It made for a brilliant, secluded "hide-out" in the city. She'd inherited it along with her new purpose in life.

Mina paused in her car to reflect on the short period of time she'd spent in the room in this little apartment as a captive. She'd been held in the exact spot where she was now holding James. She didn't like to think about those days. No one likes being held against their will. But it was only a matter of time before she proved herself worthy of the trust of her captor. She'd worked her way right out of that room and into his life as his accomplice and confidante.

Mina remembered the exact moment that had happened. It was the night Lacose had killed Jessup, his partner, to protect Mina from Jessup's attempted rape. Mina had learned Lacose's method of disposing of a body. They'd worked together to place two large trash bags over Jessup's body and connect the bags with duct tape in the middle. Then she'd helped him carry Jessup's body to the open trunk of the car. There were cameras in the parking garage, but with the trunk up and the car parked right outside the apartment, they were able to get the body in the trunk undetected.

Mina let herself in the apartment. Like she did obsessively every time she returned home, she immediately checked the door that held James. It was still locked tight. When she was first held here, she'd initially thought the lock on the door had been installed backwards, giving whoever was in the main room total control over the lock. At the same time, the person inside the room had zero control over their freedom. What she later discovered was the lock was on the outside of the door because the whole door unit had been installed backwards. The door opened out into the main room instead of into the bedroom.

Mina shook her head at this example of the strategic brilliance her kidnapper-turned-lover had possessed. The blind between the plexiglass frames had been her addition to the room, which she now opened to reveal that James was napping on the bed. Next, she lifted the plexiglass closest to her and placed the food in the middle of the glass. She locked her window back in place. She turned on the intercom.

"Wake up, Mr. Friesen!" She hit the glass, reacting to the anger she felt over this day. "It's past noon."

James jerked and his eyes flew open. He looked around in confusion. Mina assumed he had a hard time sleeping last night and was exhausted from his late-night musing. Mina sure remembered how hard it was to get used to sleeping in this place. She had once been a prisoner in this very room.

James sat up slowly and paused after swinging his legs over the edge of the bed and sitting upright.

"I have food for you," Mina said. She tapped the glass.

James stood up and looked at the food in the middle of the glass. As he approached, his window opened, and he was able to grab the food.

"Wow!" James said as he inspected the window. "How are you doing that?"

"It's remote controlled," Mina snapped. "Don't get any ideas. I control everything from out here. Also, there's a whole case of water in that pantry in the bathroom. Pace yourself, once you're out of water, you'll have to wait for me to bring it to you one at a time."

"Thank you," James said as he went in search of the water. "Did you create this plexiglass window?"

"I had help," Mina answered. She wasn't feeling too talkative at the moment. She had banked on the fact that James was an important business owner who would be reported as missing the minute he didn't show up for that meeting. Reporting him missing would trigger the chain of events that would end with Paige coming to find James and Mina capturing Paige to kill James in front of her. To Mina's knowledge, no one had reported James missing yet.

"Anyone I would know?" James asked between bites of food.

"What?" Mina looked at him blankly. She had been studying her plan. She had figured this would take a week, tops.

"Who helped you make this plexiglass contraption? Anyone I know?" James asked again.

"Oh. No one you know. But your wife pissed off quite a few people while she was here. She arrested a guy named Eric Janson for passport fraud, of all things…" Mina laughed.

James didn't join her. He looked like he didn't get the joke. Mina rolled her eyes. Paige had committed passport fraud in her attempts to flee to Canada, which had landed her in jail for a while. Ironically, after she'd had Eric arrested for that very crime. What do they call that? Projecting.

"Anyway… Eric Janson was all too happy to join my crusade to destroy Paige when he heard my plan."

"Oh, I thought you were acting alone here," James looked pensive and glanced around the room where she stood.

"Don't look so surprised. How do you think I got your unconscious body from the SUV to this room? Did you think I could carry you?"

"Well, no but I didn't think—"

"I know my limitations, James. Physical strength is one of them. The success of a plan depends on putting the right people in the right place. Eric Janson was available to provide the physical strength."

James finished his burger and fries. "Thank you for lunch."

"Ugh, that's all I need. How can you be so polite in this situation?"

"I don't know. What good is it going to do if I get mad, eh? It won't change anything."

"I need to go back to work, James. Gilly Vance does not like tardiness." Mina began to shut the wooden slats.

"Wait, you work for Gilly? You work at my company?" James asked.

"Yes, James. That was all part of the bigger plan. Goodbye for now." Mina shut off the intercom but not before she heard James exclaim an expletive.

Good, Mina thought. *I hope James gets good and mad before this is over.* She didn't want to talk herself out of following through on this plan. It would all be easier if he got spiteful with her.

The easier it will be to kill him, my dear, Lacose whispered sweetly in her ear.

"Yes," Mina agreed. This would end with James dying while Paige watched every torturous moment.

11

MINA

With a half hour before she was due back to work, Mina decided to stop and indulge in one of her guilty pleasures. She sat in the corner booth of the local Carl's Jr. and unwrapped her burger, remembering the day she'd met Eric Janson here. The day that all her plans had come together.

That day, she hadn't wanted any attention. This was no small task since she ate here on a regular basis. On the other hand, she had reasoned that if enough people could vouch for her in public, she might create an alibi, should her plan work and she needed one.

Mina had put a ball cap on over her short, black hair. She pulled it low over her eyes. Then she'd watched as the door swung open, and in walked Eric Janson. Mina had never met him personally, but she'd instantly recognized him from his mugshot. He was handsome in a young and obvious sort of way. He had short, sandy-blond hair and a neatly trimmed beard. He was tall and thin. But his dark brown eyes were piercing. The intensity of them as he scanned the little restaurant made Mina shiver involuntarily.

While she was working his case back when she was still at

the police services, she'd heard about his little sex fetish. He and his girlfriend had allowed a murderer to walk right into a hotel while they were under the front desk having sex. They'd even left a key on the counter for this guy, which enabled him to go right to the hotel room, lure a girl out there by ordering food, and then brutally murder her. Eric Janson had spent a few weeks in jail for passport fraud, but when he cooperated with the police and named Danny Jessup as the person who'd picked up the key, the police had let Eric go as promised.

Mina had told Eric to look for a black ball cap. Which is why he'd spotted her quickly and had sauntered her way with little hesitation.

Hey, he'd said flirtatiously, approval in his eyes as he sat down across from her.

Hi, I'm Mina. She'd extended her hand.

I'm Eric, he'd said, grasping her hand and holding on to it a little too long.

The reason I called you—she took back her hand.

Wait, he'd interrupted, *let me guess. You've seen me around and think I'm hot? I get that a lot. I do have a girlfriend, but she's a little freaky. She might be up for another threesome.*

I'm gonna stop you right there. I'm not looking for a date. I'm looking for revenge, Mina had stated directly, staring into the dark depth of his soulless eyes.

Lady, you got the wrong guy. I just spent time in jail not too long ago and I'm not going back. I'm not in the mood for illegal activity. Unless we're talking sex in public, of course. He'd grinned impishly.

No, that's not what this is about. Mina had held up a hand. *We have a mutual enemy. I need to eliminate her, and I have a feeling you'll help as soon as you hear who it is.*

Eric had drummed his fingers on the table. Mina thought he must have stayed out of sheer curiosity. *I'm listening.*

Paige Mynart.

Woah, really? Isn't she an officer? I don't want to mess with that.

Not anymore, Mina corrected. *Don't forget if it wasn't for Paige Mynart, you wouldn't have left Florida until you were good and ready to leave. If you even left at all.*

Yeah, that whole situation really pissed me off. But, I don't wanna kill anyone. Not even her.

You can leave that to me. Besides, I didn't say kill. I said eliminate. Mina sat up straighter in her seat, assuming her new leadership role. She wasn't as dominating as Lacose, but she knew how to pull off his authoritarian style.

Wouldn't you rather just go get a room? Eric teased with a smirk on his face.

I killed the last guy who tried to rape me, and I can do it again. The truth was, Mina hadn't killed him. Lacose had killed Jessup, defending Mina for that stunt he'd tried to pull with her. Mina had merely helped Lacose clean it up.

No one said anything about rape. You've got it all wrong. Ladies practically throw themselves at me. I don't force anything. Eric had stared at her with his hands lifted like he was surrendering to the police.

I'm terribly impressed. Is working for a woman going to be a problem here? she'd asked. *I just need someone who is physically stronger than me to do some odd jobs. It's really that simple.*

What do you need me to do? he'd asked.

That was the beginning of what Mina now called an amiable working relationship with Eric Janson.

12

JAMES

I stared toward the ceiling I knew must be somewhere over my head. With the lights off, the room was so dark—even in the middle of the day. I was tired but I could not sleep. I was exhausted, in fact. I didn't handle stress well. I never had. It was true that I used humor as a way to cope. The times in my life when I could find no humor in a situation made me feel as dark as the room I was in right now. I could feel my mind sliding toward that darkness now. I was a complexity of extremes. I was light and funny, or I was dark and sad.

Didn't take long to get here, did it, James? my brain taunted me mercilessly. *Mister-take-it-to-your-higher-power… Where's your higher power now?*

I groaned and turned onto my stomach, putting a pillow over my head. I tried to relax. I thought about meditating. I might have even said a prayer. But it was too late. The darkness had crept in. My brain boxed me mercilessly.

Whose bright idea was it to get on a plane and fly to Canada three weeks before your wife was due, you freaking idiot!

I felt hot tears of panic and defeat. There was no way out of this box room. My capturer had been hospitable so far, giving me a nice bed, bathroom, and shower. But it would only last until she lured Paige here to kill me in front of her.

Next time, maybe you could listen to your wife. She's much smarter than you, you know. Oh wait, there won't be a next time. This is it for you, buddy. Start making your peace with God!

There was no phone here to call my sponsor. There would be no way to leave to go to a meeting. I couldn't seem to stop the thoughts that spun out of control in that negative, analytical way that often left me searching for alcohol. Alcohol was a way to ease my pain and drown out the voices.

Then I heard another mocking voice. It was the voice of my inebriated father from when I was just a boy and afraid of the dark.

James, boys aren't afraid of the dark, my dad had laughed.

Okay, I'd said uncertainly but felt confused. Just because I wasn't *supposed* to be afraid didn't mean I knew how to stop. I was just a kid. *But I heard a sound...* I'd whined.

No sound you need concern yourself with, son. I'm right outside your room with your mom and nothing is happening. Dad was downright dismissive.

I'd noticed that when dad got home from work at night, he seemed tired until he drank his nightly cocktail. I didn't like it when he drank. Sometimes he would be happy, but it never lasted long. After a certain point, dad would become irritable and sometimes rude. In fact, it was like I couldn't do anything right anymore. Nothing I did in those moments fixed it or made him happy.

Be brave and go back to sleep James. Everything will be all right. You'll see in the morning. Then dad would leave me alone in the dark where I'd feel more afraid than I'd felt before.

Sometimes my older and much wiser sister would come in quietly and comfort me. Eventually, she left for college and no one missed her more than me.

I'd try to go back to sleep but I'd begun to understand that the sounds that scared me were the sounds dad made long after I was supposed to be sleeping. Almost like dad was stumbling over things and losing his balance. Some nights, he'd hit the wall as if it were the wall's fault that he fell into it.

Dad wasn't abusive. He never hit me or my mom. But as I grew up, I understood the fear of unexplained noises I had at night was the result of not knowing what dad would do at night after he'd been drinking.

As a child, it made me feel so out of control. Which is exactly how I felt right now. I wasn't in control of my surroundings, what happened next, or the future of my life.

Powerlessness is something I had learned in the program. What I didn't know was how to deal with it when there was nothing in my life I had power over. Tears formed in my eyes again. This time, I let them fall. Maybe for now, I could mourn the loss of my control and come up with a plan for how to deal with this tomorrow.

Another voice surfaced. One that sounded a little like hope. It was quiet though. So quiet I could barely hear it.

Fight, James! You're stronger than this. You'll think of a plan. Believe in yourself. I sat with that for a minute. I began to believe it. I believed in me. I could do this. Peace instantly flooded through me. The shame and blame could be so exhausting. But the peace released me to relax. I closed my eyes and fell asleep.

I'd learned the hard way we only have today. We aren't promised tomorrow.

13

PAIGE

Anna was screaming again. Paige was hiding in her closet. Her nerves were shot from the lack of sleep. Not only did Anna wake her up every hour last night, but Paige's huge belly was also making it uncomfortable for her to sleep, even if she was able. At the moment, Paige needed a little break from the anger and mood swings Anna threw. Who knew being a mom would be this hard?

Paige could have compassion for Anna when she had nightmares. In fact, Paige had her fair share of nightmares during her childhood as well. Only there had been no one to comfort her when she was a child.

This wasn't one of Anna's nightmares, though. At the moment, Anna was throwing herself on the floor in a tantrum because Paige had given her cereal instead of toaster waffles. Instead of dealing with it, Paige had ignored Anna's spoiled behavior and walked out of the room.

Her phone started ringing. She wiped the tears from her exhausted eyes and looked at her caller ID. It was Stephen Wilton, Anna's birth father.

"Stephen? Oh, thank God!" Paige breathed a sigh of relief.

"Paige? Are you okay?" he asked.

"No, I'm not."

"What's happening?" Concern was evident in Stephen's voice.

"Anna is on the floor, as we speak, throwing a tantrum because I gave her cereal instead of waffles," Paige sniffed, tears threatening to fall again.

"Sounds like she needs a time out," Stephen's voice was stern and matter of fact.

"Oh, right." It was such a simple suggestion, and yet Paige was coming to realize she knew nothing about discipline. Her own mother had not disciplined her. She'd never really been around kids before she had one. Paige had gone from having an infant to having a willful three-year-old in what felt like a matter of minutes. She hadn't had time to prepare.

"Tell you what," Stephen said. "I was calling to say I'm in the area and wanted to pick up Anna. Would that help?"

"Yes!"

"In the meantime, maybe James could help you with Anna?" Stephen suggested. "I'm about an hour away."

Paige tried not to feel offended by Stephen's hint that she couldn't handle Anna on her own. How could she feel offended when she knew he was right? Instead, she started crying and blurted the thing that she'd been worrying about most. The real reason she knew she was struggling with Anna's temper.

"James has gone missing."

There was a pause. "What do you mean, he's gone missing?" Stephen asked.

"I mean, I haven't heard from him since he got off the plane yesterday afternoon," Paige felt fear spilling out of her through her verbal word vomit.

"Oh no, Paige. Not again. I'm so sorry." His words were meant to comfort her. They didn't.

She felt her anxiety kick up a notch. "It's not the same as

before, Stephen," Paige snapped. "He went on a business trip to Canada, and he called to let me know he had landed. That was the last time I heard from him. I'm so worried. What if something has happened to him?"

There was another pause. "Paige, you know he does this. Maybe he's feeling the stress of the babies coming and has—"

"Relapsed? Is that what you were going to say, Stephen?" Paige heard her voice rise.

"Well, yes, actually," he said matter-of-factly. His voice held no apology for his assumption.

"When I talked to him last, he was happy. He was planning to be back in two days. In fact, I'm supposed to pick him up from the airport tomorrow morning. If he's not answering his phone, there's a reason," she insisted. "And it's not that he fell off the wagon. He's happy now."

"Okay, okay," Stephen said. "What were you hoping I could do?"

"Nothing, yet." Paige lowered her voice. "I'm sorry, Stephen. There's nothing you can do. You asked, and that's what's happening. I'll go to the airport tomorrow morning, and he'll probably get off the flight and all will be fine."

Stephen was a US Marshal. It's what kept him away as often as he was. In truth, Stephen could go to Canada and launch an investigation into James' whereabouts tomorrow. Paige just wasn't ready to ask him, nor did she think he would agree. Besides, reporting James missing would make it official and Paige wasn't ready for that either. It would be like giving in to her worst fear. The truth of Stephen's words bounced around in her brain. Stephen could be right. It was possible that James had fallen off the wagon again.

"I hope you're right. How about I keep Anna all day so you can take a break and get some rest?" Stephen asked.

Paige agreed, hung up the phone, and composed herself. She walked back into the dining room to find Anna quietly eating her cheerios. Maybe walking out of the room and ignoring Anna's fit had been the right way to handle it.

"Hi mom." Anna looked up at her with big eyes. She was swinging her feet that dangled over the chair where she sat. To Paige, she seemed tall for her age. Maybe she had hit a growth spurt.

"Thank you for sitting in your chair and eating your breakfast. No more throwing fits or you'll go in time out, do you understand?" Paige had conjured up her most stern voice.

Anna sat up taller and her eyes got big. Time out must have been a hated discipline from her dad because Anna nodded solemnly. It was hard for Paige to remember that before they had lost a year with Anna, Anna had been with Stephen, and he had already instilled disciplinary tactics. Paige needed to remember it didn't make her weak to reach out for help from him, it made her a stronger parent.

After all, successful coparenting was just that, right? Combining the best parenting strategies from each parent to raise a strong, independent child. At least, that's what Paige thought must be the case. Anna wasn't going to raise herself. If she tried, she'd turn out like Paige. With her mostly absentee mom, Paige had a rough transition into adulthood.

Less than an hour later, Stephen knocked at the front door. Paige had bathed Anna and let her choose her clothes. Anna didn't match perfectly but she'd been so decisive, Paige had let her have her way. She didn't think things like clothes were something to fight about.

"Who's at the front door?" Paige asked her.

Anna looked hesitant. "Mama Carley didn't let me answer the door by myself," Anna whispered.

"Right," Paige said. "That's actually a really good rule. I'll go with you, but I'm pretty sure it's a safe person on the other side."

"Okay," Anna said cheerfully.

When Anna saw Stephen on the other side of the door, she squealed and flew into his arms. "Daddy!"

Stephen dropped down, picked her up off the floor, and spun her around. "I've missed you! How's my little girl?"

"Good!" Anna said, her arms around his neck, hugging him tightly.

"Have you been a good girl for mommy?" Stephen asked as he settled her on his lap.

"Nope," she admitted, shaking her head, her eyes big.

"What? Why not?" Stephen's face became stern.

"I dunno," Anna said as she shook her head, her blond curls bouncing.

"You be good to mommy, Anna. Or the next time I come to see you, we won't be able to do fun things."

Anna gasped and slid off his lap. She went over and hugged Paige's leg. "I'm sorry, mommy."

"I forgive you, Anna." Paige awkwardly squatted down and hugged Anna.

Anna kissed Paige on the cheek.

"What do you have planned for this little one today?" Paige asked Stephen while looking at Anna. She really was a beautiful child. Her blond curly hair resembled her dad's, and she had blue eyes that matched his. If Paige didn't know better, she might wonder if Anna was even hers. But Paige knew that strong-willed independence in Anna came straight from her own heart.

"It's a surprise!" Stephen said. Then he put his hand over his mouth and whispered the word. "Zoo!"

Anna shrieked loudly. "I heard you!" She jumped around excitedly.

"Thank you, Stephen. You couldn't have come at a better time, really."

"Yeah," he said as his eyes grew serious. "Keep me posted on you know who."

Paige appreciated Stephen keeping her concern quiet in front of Anna. Anna was advanced beyond her three years. Paige knew because she'd had all sorts of psychological tests done on Anna after they'd found her. It turned out Anna was a mini genius. She could read Easy Readers already. Her vocabulary was advanced. And there was a good chance she threw fits because she was under stimulated and a bit bored. That gave Paige pause. How should she stimulate a three-year-old child? She needed to experiment with that one. However, because she lacked the energy during the pregnancy, this task often fell to James.

"Bye, mom!" Anna said. She hugged Paige one more time, took her dad's hand, and walked out the door with him.

Paige shut the door, feeling relief. First on the agenda was a nice hot bubble bath. Next, she would take a nap. Somewhere in there, she'd say a prayer for her husband. Would he really have failed his sobriety test on day number one?

No matter how much Paige tried to relax into the bath, this question stayed on her mind. As she got dressed, she attempted to give the worry to a higher power in prayer. But as she attempted to relax and burrow into the warm, thick comforter on her bed, sleep was elusive. The best she could do was lay still and rest picturing the vivid, twinkling blue eyes of her handsome husband. With eyes closed, she said another prayer that he would come back home to her unharmed.

14

MINA

After a long and boring day at the office, Mina was finally back home. *Back home.* She contemplated those words for a minute. No other place where she'd lived had felt like home. Not until she'd come here. The place where she'd found love and still saw remnants of it everywhere she turned. She had let her lease lapse on the place where she'd lived before the event that changed her forever. This apartment was her home now.

She eagerly fell onto the sofa, which she had shoved against the wall. The couch was the only comfortable piece of furniture in the room. Mina didn't need comfort, she needed efficiency. The main room was an open floor layout—not in the trendy way. It was just one big room with cheap, thin carpeting on the floor in the living room and linoleum in the dining room and kitchen. The dining room table had become her office desk, complete with a computer and high-tech equipment left over from the last mission.

She sat up taller, perching on the edge of the sofa as she turned on the six o'clock nightly news and watched for the entire hour. She was aware that she was ignoring her prisoner at the moment. It had been twenty-four hours since she'd abducted James and there was still nothing on the news. Similar to James' no show at the office meeting, no one seemed concerned enough to report his disappearance.

As Mina got up to fix James a sandwich, she felt rage boiling under the surface. She mindlessly set the sandwich down and stood in front of her white board. She began looking over the plans. If no one was looking for James, then the rest of her plan simply would not work. She turned and opened the wooden blinds that separated her from James. Like every other time when she'd opened the blinds, she found him lounging on the bed. There was no other furniture for him to lounge on. She supposed that was why.

Mina slammed the palm of her hand against the plexiglass. "Hey!" she exclaimed loudly.

What had gotten into her? She was usually so composed. Sure, there were problems that bothered her in the past, but she could usually get over them quickly. She was typically even tempered and was able to logically reason problems out without even talking to anyone else. She was the master of her emotions. Until now. All her plans were threatening to unravel.

"Hey," James looked up, surprise on his face. "How was your day?"

"Why isn't anyone looking for you, James?" she spat out angrily.

"What do you mean?" His face looked blank.

"I mean you've been here for two days, and no one is looking for you. They don't seem to care that you missed the meeting at work. There's nothing on the news about your disappearance." Mina hit the glass again to punctuate each of her words. "What. Are. You. Not. Telling. Me?"

"Oh, that." James sat up and swung his legs over the edge of the bed, looking dejected. "Disappearing was a thing I did a lot in my past. No-showing meetings wasn't uncommon for me. I've changed, but no one here would know that."

"Why?" Mina exploded. "Why aren't you a responsible human being?"

"I'm an alcoholic," James said simply. "I'm in recovery now, but it was a pretty big problem for a while. I tended to isolate from the people who care about me. Or hole up in the same bar for days. Disappearing was normal behavior for me in the past."

Mina shouted an expletive. She flailed her arms in the air and turned a circle which looked like a full-body adult fit.

"What about Paige? Aren't you two married? Shouldn't she be worried about you?"

Before James could answer, there was a loud knock at the door. Mina put a finger to her lips, forgetting for a moment that she controlled the sound. She quickly dropped the blinds.

Mina checked the peephole. Vanessa Ireland stood on the other side of the door. Vanessa was Eric Janson's very pretty girlfriend. The last time Mina had seen Vanessa was after Paige had made contact with her and convinced Vanessa to come back to Canada. She and Eric had flown out of the country in order to avoid the murder they had played a part in. Mina had always wondered how both of them had avoided accessory to murder charges with that stunt they'd pulled in the hotel—literally leaving a key for a murderer while they messed around under the front desk. Paige had Vanessa arrested. But with no evidence, they couldn't hold her.

Mina felt her blood pressure go up, knowing Eric had told Vanessa where Mina's secret apartment was. She had no patience for chit chat and determined to get rid of her quickly. Mina answered the door a crack and peered out.

"Vanessa?" Mina asked through a small crack.

Vanessa kicked the door open with unexpected force, knocking Mina on her bottom.

"Vanessa!" Mina exclaimed in surprise.

Vanessa was through the door now. She slammed it quickly. Taking advantage of Mina on the ground, Vanessa jumped on her, her legs straddling Mina's body. Vanessa grabbed Mina's wrist and pushed her down to the ground, pinning Mina's hands to the side of her head on the ground. Vanessa's face hovered above Mina's and her body weight rested on top of Mina's.

"Where's Eric?" Vanessa hissed. She was so close to Mina's face, Mina could feel her hot breath. It smelled like bubblegum.

"Why would I know?" Mina asked, genuinely baffled.

"Because you're sleeping with him!" Vanessa accused her. She slapped Mina hard across the face.

"Why on earth would you think that?" Mina gasped. Her jaw stung from the impact. Her eyes watered.

"You didn't deny it," Vanessa looked smug and angry at the same time. She looked like she had just solved the crime of the century.

"Get off me and look around, you crazy psycho! Do you see him here?" Mina began to struggle but Vanessa had the upper hand and more weight on her which made it easy to keep Mina pinned. Vanessa punched Mina's face. This time pain exploded behind Mina's eye.

"Deny it one more time," Vanessa hissed. "I dare you."

"I wouldn't touch your disgusting, disease-infested boyfriend with a ten-foot pole." Mina spat out the cliché with as much force as her pain-filled face would enable.

Miraculously, Vanessa jumped up, setting Mina free. "I heard you talking to someone. He's here." Vanessa began scanning the room and opening the bedroom doors. She got to James' room and tried the door.

James must have heard the commotion. He pounded on the door at the exact moment Vanessa tried the door.

"Hey," he yelled. "Help, she's holding me hostage!"

Vanessa jumped back in surprise. She turned in time to see Mina holding a gun. It was inches from Vanessa's head.

"That doesn't sound like Eric," Vanessa whispered. "What are you doing? Who is that?"

"That's not your concern," Mina stated with an equally quiet voice.

"You're right." Vanessa tried a new tactic. Her voice sounded logical and rational now. "This really *is* none of my business. I'll just go."

"Too late." Mina put her finger on the trigger and pulled it at Vanessa's forehead. She watched Vanessa's eyes register shock and fear at the same time. Her head jerked back, then her eyelids slid closed. Vanessa's body went limp, and she fell to the floor. Mina watched the red blood begin to pour out of Vanessa's head onto the linoleum.

The front door opened and slammed shut quickly, and Mina turned around in surprise. Her gun swung around with her as she turned. It was Eric. A thought flashed in her mind—this was all Eric's fault. If it hadn't been for him, Vanessa would still be alive.

"Noooo!" he yelled when he spotted what was left of his beautiful girlfriend bleeding on the floor. He rushed over and put his hands against her cheeks. He felt for a pulse. "What have you done?"

"Don't move!" Mina screamed.

Eric froze, straightened slowly, and put his hands in the air. "Put the gun down, Mina. Let's just talk."

"It's too late for talking, Eric. You have a mess to clean up," Mina tilted her head toward Vanessa, who was lying on the floor with blood pooling under her head from the gunshot wound.

Eric was crying now. Fear showed in his eyes as he forced himself to look at Mina. "What do you mean *I* have to clean it up? That's my girlfriend!"

"Exactly what I said. You're the one who let her find me.

Because of you, she heard our prisoner. I couldn't let her go, even if she hadn't attacked me."

"She attacked you?" Eric whispered. He looked back down at his lifeless girlfriend.

Mina used her free hand to gesture to the eye, which she could feel was already beginning to swell and was probably already turning blue.

"Yeah, you look really messed up," Eric gawked at her. "Vanessa did that? My Vanessa?"

"Yeah. And now you get to help me dispose of her."

"But why?" he whined.

"Because you couldn't keep your zipper up. She came at me because she thought I was cheating with you."

Eric's face colored.

"Don't say a word," Mina said as she backed up to a drawer that held trash bags and duct tape. "You disgust me."

"Me? I'm not the one who killed an innocent woman," Eric argued.

"Yes. You did." Mina threw two trash bags at him. Then she threw duct tape at him. "Put her feet in one bag and cover her head with the second bag. Then, tape the two bags together in the middle."

Eric did as he was commanded. Mina held the gun the whole time.

"Throw her over your shoulder. I'm gonna pop the trunk to my car and you're going to throw her in the trunk. Then I'm gonna join you in the car. You try anything and you're next."

Eric obeyed every command.

Mina had done this before and gotten away with it. Since the last time, she'd scoped out the cameras in the parking garage. She knew all the angles and knew how to avoid being seen. It's how she'd been able to come and go the way she had without ever being noticed. As far as the landlord knew, Lacose was still paying the rent. Since she paid in cash, the landlord was none the wiser.

With her gun pointed at Eric, she made him drive. The sun set earlier in fall evenings, and it was getting darker by the minute. Mina was silent from the passenger seat. So was Eric. That's how she knew it wasn't Eric who said the words that echoed in her head.

You know you'll have to kill him. It was the voice of the man she loved.

Mina stifled a gasp. Emotion flooded through her body. How she missed him.

He knows too much, and you just killed his girlfriend, the voice continued.

Mina's heart hammered in her chest, and she casually looked in the back seat. The voice was so audible in her mind, she thought she actually might have heard it. She half thought she would see Ludwig sitting in the back seat when she turned around. But she didn't have to see him to recognize him. Her heart yearned for him.

"What is it?" Eric's fearful voice broke into the semi-silent car. "Is someone following us?"

"No, Eric, just drive," Mina commanded, holding the gun steady in his direction.

Kill him, Lacose's voice sounded in her ear. Mina imagined in this moment he was still here with her. *You don't need him. You're strong enough to do it on your own.*

It was well after dark when they made it to the Red River, and Mina knew the spot where they wouldn't be seen.

After Eric helped her dump Vanessa's body, he turned to face Mina, a mixture of relief and grief on his face. She could see he thought the worst was over. That's why he didn't see it coming. Mina shot him point blank through his forehead. His body fell backward into the river from the force of the gunshot. He floated in the same direction Vanessa's body had floated.

"Good riddance," Mina mumbled.

Now she'd cleaned up the mess Eric had created and made sure there was no trail of crazy people left that would come back to her. There was no one else on Earth to keep her from completing her plan. As she got back in her car, she heard his voice again. She'd do anything to hear that voice again and again.

Good job, my clever minx.

15

JAMES

I'd heard everything. Mina had left the intercom on. I'd heard the woman come in. I'd heard her fighting with Mina. I'd heard the gunshot. Then, I'd heard the silent stillness. I knew what had happened. Mina had killed that woman. It sounded like a reaction. She hadn't planned it.

If I'd had any doubts over whether Mina was capable of murder, I didn't anymore. At that point, my whole body began to shake. Mina was going to kill me. I had no doubt. My best move in that moment was to be quiet and still. I was hoping Mina had forgotten about me while that was happening.

Then I heard a guy come in and start freaking out. She must have turned the gun on him because he changed his tone real fast. He did everything she asked. Then I heard them leave together.

I lay on the bed, my body curled into the fetal position. It was only a matter of time before Mina returned. I wiped the tears that formed. I felt momentarily paralyzed. Then something in my brain clicked.

It's only a matter of time before she returns!

I flew into action. I looked under the bed for a piece of a bed frame I could screw off the bed in order to hit the plexiglass. There wasn't much space under the bed. No luck.

As I had every time I'd assumed Mina was gone, I inspected the plexiglass contraption. This time, I hit it with my palm. Nothing happened. I made a fist and hit it with all my strength. I howled in pain but did it again two more times. Just in case. Nothing was happening. I tried to push it up, but it seemed locked in place.

You're wasting time, my brain snapped. I stopped touching the plexiglass. I took a slow step back.

Doing the same thing over and over again but wishing for a different result is insanity. I'd heard that somewhere before. My eyes fell on the lock on the door, curious that it was backwards. Had Mina had the doorknob changed as part of her master plan? She must have.

It was a Kwikset security cove. I could see a tiny hole in the lock. I'd messed with these on many a construction site. All I needed was a thin nail. Inspired, I walked quickly to the bathroom and shut the door. I didn't have the courage to ask Mina if there was a camera in the bathroom. Surely, she was giving me privacy in there. Though I didn't have the luxury of assuming anything.

Taking things apart was what I did best. I had started that when I was a child. From as far back as I could remember, I would take toys apart just to learn how to put them back together again. If they didn't go back together, I'd try it again and again. On rare occasions, if I found myself not succeeding, I'd hide the toy somewhere, hoping no one ever found it. As a kid, I got the impression my parents did okay financially but did not tolerate waste.

Without warning, the one memory of when my dad had caught me taking something apart came back to me. That something was his transistor radio. What I didn't know is that it was an old model radio that had been in the family for some time and passed down to my dad. He had planned to pass it down to me, but I'd let my curiosity get the best of me before that ever happened. When my mom was making dinner one night, I had climbed up on my dad's desk and had taken it off a high shelf. I'd seen him messing with it and was curious to know how the sound came out.

Only, I never figured it out. I didn't have time to. I was so engrossed in my project, I didn't even notice when my dad threw open the door. He had lifted me up off the floor where I'd been kneeling over my bed studying the parts. Suddenly, I was up against the wall. Had I been eight or nine?

What the hell are you doing? That's mine! he'd thundered at me. I was so scared, I couldn't speak.

Well, answer me! He shook me once and pinned me against the wall again. My feet dangled helplessly in the air. I felt truly powerless.

I wanted to see how it worked, I whispered.

Speak up, son! Own your actions, he commanded.

Instead, I'd started to cry. He'd set me gruffly on the floor then. *Okay, put it back together. Show me how it works.*

It was the longest night of my life. He made me stay up for hours past bedtime. My mom begged him to let me go to bed.

He needs to go to sleep. He has school tomorrow, she'd said, clutching his arm.

Oh, no! He needs to figure this out tonight. It was important enough for him to steal it and disassemble it. He's gonna show me how he can make it work again.

I hadn't had dinner. I was so exhausted. My eyes were drooping. When I finally got it back together, it looked right but still didn't work. I tried to hand it back to my dad.

Oh no, that's yours now. It would've been yours eventually. But now that it doesn't work, I have no use for it. Congratulations on inheriting a broken family heirloom. He'd left the room in a huff.

I'd crawled into bed after that. It had taken me hours to get to sleep. The guilt and shame over my actions was devastating. I cried quietly so my dad couldn't hear me. I pushed the radio under my bed. Before I finally nodded off, I determined I would fix that radio someday. I did fix it.

Just like I would fix this situation now. No one was coming for me. It was all up to me. I didn't have any time to wallow in self-pity. Mina had to know I'd heard what happened. Which meant she would likely kill me when she came back.

I dropped to my knees and looked closely at all the cabinets. They were cheap and manufactured from a facility. The hinges had hex-drive sheet metal screws in them which would be too thick to maneuver into the door, even if I could find a way to unscrew them.

Still, I looked, feeling encouraged. I looked for a good hour. I just needed to find a thin nail fast and break out of here. Tonight, if possible.

"James, are you still here?" Mina called with a self-appreciating laugh as she came in the door.

How long had she been gone? An hour or two? I really had no sense of time here.

I didn't want to give away that I'd heard what happened earlier, so I pretended not to hear her now. There was also the unknown question about the camera situation.

I quickly hopped to my feet and exited the bathroom. I plopped down innocently on the bed. I didn't want her to be suspicious that I'd been looking for a way out. I could spend the night coming up with a plan to get out of here. *If* she let me live that long.

I could hear the sound of a push broom against the floor. There was a steady movement. Then I had a sickening realization. Mina was cleaning. She must be cleaning up the blood.

Mina had left with one person who was alive and had come back alone. It didn't have to mean anything. I hoped that the person went his own way after helping Mina dispose of the body. But I knew better. The man had sounded so distraught over the other woman's death. Mina didn't seem to tolerate anything less than loyalty to her and her plan.

The more I thought about my situation, the more fear crept into my heart. I began to shake. Panic hit me hard. My brain clouded with dark thoughts full of despair and grief.

No one is coming for you, James, my brain taunted.

I turned my body away from the door and plexiglass window and stared at the wall and baseboards. That was it! If I somehow took apart the baseboard, there should be a nail there. Most likely, it would be the size I needed. Hope soared in me again. I just needed time. I had no clue how I would take apart the baseboard without tools, but I would find a way.

16

JAMES

"Dinner time, James," Mina opened the slat and put a sandwich in the window. She closed the panel and opened mine.

She must have cleaned that mess up quickly. I was still pretending to sleep. But then my stomach growled loudly, betraying me. I was too hungry to sleep right now. My stomach told me it was past dinner time and it was later in the evening than I usually eat. I supposed I should be grateful she remembered to feed me after her killing spree.

Mina giggled. It was an odd sound. One I didn't expect. Stubbornly, I was lying with my back to the panel.

"Come on, James. I know you must be hungry. And I don't think you're sleeping either. Please eat." Mina's voice had a pleading tone.

I decided to take pity on her, though I wasn't sure why. I'd thought long and hard about my approach with her. I could do this the hard way, make her angry, and end it all sooner. Or I could try to be her friend. Maybe I could talk her into letting me go. It was a long shot, but I had to keep in mind that she hadn't always been this way. She had to have been a decent human being before. Maybe I could appeal to her humanity.

I moved slowly, pretending to just wake up. I stirred, then I sat up and stretched a little. I blinked owlishly, then rubbed my eyes. I got up and took the food from the window.

"Cut the act, James, I know you heard everything." Mina averted her eyes from mine. She looked sadly at the floor. Most likely at the spot she had been cleaning up. Did she actually feel remorse over her actions?

I took the sandwich and sat down on the bed. I shrugged. "I might have heard a gunshot."

"Oh." Mina's eyes filled with despair. "I didn't mean to do that."

Again, I shrugged, pretending to be casual. "It's really not my business. You have a plan." I waved a sandwich at the whiteboard behind her that she'd been so proud of.

"That wasn't a part of my plan. She came out of nowhere. She attacked. I just reacted." Mina put her hands on her face and sank to the couch.

I watched her with surprise. Was this an act? "Hey, Mina. Are you okay?"

Mina looked up at me for a second, then up at the ceiling. "I don't know," she admitted. "I think this has all gotten out of hand."

"It's not too late to back out, Mina. If you let me go right now, I'll walk out of here and never say a word. Everyone makes mistakes."

"What?" Mina snapped and looked at me with sudden anger. "No, I'm in control. I know what I'm doing with *you*. You are part of the plan. *They* weren't part of the plan."

"They?" I asked quietly. I finished my sandwich, working to swallow the lump in my throat.

Mina put her face on her hands again. "When Eric walked in after I shot Vanessa, I knew I would have to take care of him too."

I knew what she wasn't saying here. In the same way she

would have no choice but to take care of me. But then, she'd already told me that part of her plan.

"I've made mistakes too, Mina. Big ones. Ones that cost me relationships and landed me in jail. Later on, my mistakes led me to rehab."

"Bet you never killed anyone," Mina said. Tears filled her eyes.

"Wouldn't you call that self-defense?" I asked. Making an effort to bond with a murderer turned my stomach but I couldn't help but feel like the more she thought I understood her, the longer she might keep me alive.

"Yes," she whispered. Her eyes had taken on a far-away look and I knew she was remembering the past.

As I watched her, I felt a chilly realization. This wasn't the first time she'd killed someone.

"Why did you make them? *Your* mistakes," Mina asked, snapping out of her trance. She crept closer.

"I'm an alcoholic. It's genetic."

"That's it? It's genetic? If it's a lost cause, why even go to rehab? Genetically, you'd just start back up again, right?" Mina challenged me.

"Genetically, if I start, I won't be able to stop. It's my higher power who gives me the strength to stay sober. Once I understand that I'm powerless and give my control to my God, I don't have any desire to drink or do drugs."

"That's a cop-out, right? I mean what if you decide to start drinking again? Does that mean your God, or higher power, has failed you?" There was an edge in her eyes. She clearly didn't like all this talk about God.

I was silent for a minute, thinking. "No, it means I took back control. I let the fear, despair, or sadness control me instead of giving it to God." In that moment, I knew I needed to put my current situation in God's hands. I hadn't done that yet. Whether I lived through the night or lost my life tonight, it wasn't mine to control in the first place. Just like I couldn't control Mina.

She scoffed at me and sat down on the floor, cross-legged.

"What about you, Mina? Isn't there anything you struggle with and wish you could let go of?" I asked. I wanted to understand what was at the root of all this.

"Loneliness," Mina whispered. For half a second, Mina's eyes were sad. She looked so vulnerable.

Through the plexiglass, I almost missed what she said.

"Some days I feel so lonely, I could—"

"Die." I got up off the bed and stood at the plexiglass window. "Yeah, I used to call it boredom, but it was loneliness for me too."

"But then you found Paige and got married, blah, blah, blah…" Mina pretended to gag herself.

"Yeah, all that happened but I had to get real with myself first. In rehab, I was alone a lot. It was uncomfortable at first because I hated being alone with my sober thoughts. I hated myself. My thoughts were torturous. Some days they still are." I shuddered.

"Yeah?" Mina asked. She looked like she understood me. "What changed?"

"I started running and exercising. Hated that too when I first started, now it's mine. It gives me a nice natural high. And I went to group therapy and sessions with a counselor. You know anything about codependency?" I asked.

Mina shrugged. "I guess I never thought it was a big deal."

I nodded. "It is. Very big. Life and death. Codependency is like a silent death. I'd wager many suicides occur because of codependency. The rest of us, well, we hold so many things close to us, the pain practically kills us, or we want to die. Well, I had to deal with that, some past childhood stuff, and I came out a better person."

Mina snorted. "If only you knew what happened to me

growing up. There are some childhood things you can't get past."

"Like abuse?" I asked.

Mina was silent but narrowed her eyes skeptically.

"Yeah, me too. I had some of that in my childhood. The thing about truly terrible things that happen to us as children is that we get to choose what we do with it as adults. We can let it define us, or we can overcome it. Bad things happen to everyone. We are in control of who we become as a result—good or bad."

"Sounds too good to be true, James. Too simplified. I bet you'll drink again someday." Mina grinned wickedly. "If you live that long." She stood up suddenly and slammed the slats down on the plexiglass window so I could no longer see her.

I lie back on the bed again and stared at the ceiling, wondering what I'd said to close her off. I knew I wasn't perfect and hated to think that's what I'd portrayed. Still, this conversation had given me a lot to think about. I'd self-discovered a lot as I'd talked. I felt grateful I'd come so far. Even if my life ended right here, in a locked room.

I said a silent prayer to my higher power to deliver me from evil in the form of Mina Martin.

17

MINA

He's lying to you! His angry voice hissed in Mina's ear.

One minute Mina was talking to James, letting her guard fall, allowing herself to be lulled into his false insinuations of friendship. She had actually begun to believe she and James might be similar.

Then she heard his voice, the voice of the man she loved, and she realized her stupid mistake. She could never be friends with this man she'd captured. And she would never be at peace until she had murdered him the same way his love had murdered hers.

She tossed and turned in bed that night, unable to sleep. Sometimes she questioned how she had gotten where she was now. Other times, like tonight, she berated herself for her stupid, idealistic thoughts. James had been lying to her to get free. It was a ploy. There was no need for her to feel guilty or ashamed of her actions. James was the key to her peace. A life for a life. It was the only thing that made sense to her.

As she was lying in bed, she could sense a strong, loving presence. Then she felt him wrap his arms around her. He stroked her hair. She felt her body relax into his. She imagined the warmth she'd felt every time he'd been around.

Only then was she able to close her eyes and fall asleep in the arms of the man she loved. Even if he only visited her at night, his presence comforted her and encouraged her to keep going.

You're so close, Mina. You can't stop now. Paige must pay. His soft, soothing words inspired her to stay with her mission. No matter what. For him.

Mina smiled with contentment as she snuggled down into the warm comforter on the bed where they had last been together.

"James will die," she whispered with a content smile, reassuring herself of the plan as she fell asleep.

18

PAIGE

Paige sat at the baggage claim and wiped her tears. At first, she thought she could catch her tears as they fell, and no one would notice. Then the tears came gushing in a torrent. She'd been at the airport for over two hours.

James didn't get off the plane. Foolishly, she thought maybe she'd missed him, so she waited with the plane full of people who were looking for their luggage. She looked for James' luggage. She looked until the last person picked up her luggage and left the airport. James did not have luggage on the flight.

This was no oversight. It wasn't like she was at the wrong terminal. This town had such a small airport, all luggage came to the same place, staggered based on when flights came in. Paige stared without seeing the empty terminal.

With shaking hands, she pulled out her phone. She dialed J. Jackson, her old detective buddy from Canada. Only, she didn't call the Police Service of Winnipeg, she called his personal cell phone. He answered on the second ring.

"Paige?" he sounded breathless. "How's it going, eh?"

"Hi, Jackson," Paige sighed. She tried to control the wobble in her voice. She could not.

"Hey, you okay?" he asked.

"Not really. I'm calling because I need a favor." This time she just let the tears fall.

"Sounds serious," he replied. "Is it police related? If so, you should really call the station—"

"No, I don't want to report anything officially. It's just that you helped me out so much before. I wondered if you could give me advice."

"I can try."

"James flew back to Canada and—"

"Wait, James is out of rehab? Last I heard, he'd checked himself into rehab or something. Or maybe that was a rumor? It's been over six months since we last talked, Paige. Why don't you start at the beginning?" he suggested.

"You're correct. After James gave up my safe house position, he went to rehab. Then he came back for me. He's been clean and sober ever since. Only, he got on a plane two days ago to do some business in Canada. I haven't heard from him since."

There was a long silence on the other end. It almost sounded intentional. Rude even.

Finally, Jackson spoke. "Look, Paige. I hate to be the one to state the obvious, but maybe James isn't missing. Maybe he just doesn't want to be found."

Paige inhaled sharply. "So, you don't want to help me?"

"If you file a missing person report through the police service, we have no choice but to act on it. But I will tell you, we're in the middle of another murder case. A body just washed up on the shore of the Red River again. I won't have time to go get James again and throw him in a cell to sober him up."

Jackson was referencing the time not so long ago when Paige had been put into protective custody while under house arrest. During that time, men had beaten and bound James until James had given up her location. Tied up and in a weakened state of mind from drinking and doing drugs, James had told them what they'd wanted to know. She would never know why they didn't kill James after he gave the information, but she could only be grateful they hadn't.

"Got it," Paige said through clenched teeth. "I really called because I wondered if you'd seen him or heard from him in the past two days."

"I haven't heard anything at all. I didn't even know he was in town," Jackson told her.

"Okay, I'll consider putting in a police report," she said. She knew her voice sounded as sad as she felt.

"Okay. Hey, I've gotta go. The new Chief of Police is calling me. They might have an ID on a body," he said.

Paige could hear the excitement in his voice. Some days, she missed that thrill of the chase too. She had been a pretty good investigator. But she looked down at her large stomach and felt content right where she was. Minus the fact that she was missing her husband right now.

She started to hang up the phone when his final words halted her actions.

"Paige? I'll let you know if I hear anything. But guard your heart. You might not like how this turns out, eh?"

She thanked him, hung up the phone, and sobbed into her hands. She tried so hard to remember the discussion she'd had with James before he left. The one where he'd given her advice to trust her higher power. What had he said?

Look, bad things do happen. But they don't just happen to you or me. They happen to everyone. But the strong ones overcome. That's us. We're overcomers.

James liked to point out we are powerless over other people and could only control ourselves. Paige's control over her own actions was slipping fast. She was sobbing in an airport, and she didn't care who saw her.

19

JACKSON

"We've got an ID on our Red River Raven," a voice called out. It was Mazy, the new crime analyst.

There was nothing wrong with Mazy per se, but she was no Mina. Mazy drove Detective J. Jackson a little crazy. She liked to give murder victims and dead women names like they were straight out of an Agatha Christie novel. He'd told her it wasn't necessary, but she'd frowned at him without clear understanding. He gathered that she either had a morbid sense of humor or she was out of touch with reality. She was a looker, though. He'd give her that. Her shoulder-length jet-black hair, big brown eyes, and red kissable lips drew Jackson to her. He would be lying if he said he'd never thought about what it would be like to kiss her.

Still, Jackson rushed to her side. Was she wearing perfume? It tickled his nose in the most tantalizing way. Impatiently, Jackson looked at the screen, reading over Mazy's shoulder. The chief and several co-workers had gathered around.

"Vanessa Ireland?" Jackson's voice held the surprise he'd felt. He'd been one of the first detectives on the scene but couldn't ID her immediately. She'd been shot in the forehead and had floated in the river for at least twelve hours. Even though her body had been wrapped in a trash bag, she was bloated beyond recognition.

What Jackson did recognize was the way Vanessa's body had been wrapped up. It reminded him of another victim who had washed up on shore a few years ago. But the connection didn't make sense. They'd determined the man who'd killed that person was the Deliver and Dash Killer, Ludwig Lacose. He was lying in a morgue right now. Jackson had seen his dead body with his own eyes.

What he knew of Vanessa Ireland was about her slight involvement in that Deliver and Dash case from years ago. The Deliver and Dash case appeared to be mixed into this somehow, but Jackson couldn't fathom the connection. Vanessa had been cleared from any involvement with the murder after she'd cooperated with the police. Her boyfriend, Eric Janson, was a different story. Though he'd been cleared too, Jackson never quite believed he was completely innocent of conspiring with the killer.

"We've got another body!" a dispatcher across the room called out. She held a phone in her hand, clearly indicating there had been a call-in. "Fished out of the Red River."

"Betcha twenty bucks it's Eric Janson," he murmured to Mazy, who was still staring at the dispatcher with shock on her face.

"Eric Janson…" Mazy quickly typed in his name.

"Eric Allen Janson…" Jackson corrected. He should be running off to inspect the body. But something held him here a moment longer.

Her lips moved as she read aloud the paragraph on Eric Janson. "Eric Janson fled to Florida before he was officially cleared from the investigation during the Deliver and Dash murders. He and his girlfriend, Vanessa Ireland, were having sex under the check-in desk at the time the Deliver and Dash murderer came into the hotel, grabbed the hotel key from the desk, and let himself into the hotel room." She stopped reading and looked at Jackson, whose eyes had fixated on her lips as they read. "They were having sex!"

Jackson nodded but didn't trust himself to speak. He watched her face redden slightly and her mouth pop open in shock.

"Truly?" she asked.

"Would *you* lie about such a thing?" he smirked. His eyes landed on her lips again as they settled into a straight line, making a heart shape.

Her raven hair brushed her shoulders and swished from side to side as she shook her head. The smell of her perfume made him light-headed.

"I gotta go," Jackson said abruptly. He put a hand on her shoulder and patted it twice, letting it trail down her arm. He dropped his hand and clutched it tightly by his side like it had a mind of its own and he needed to get it under control. What the hell was the matter with him? He was practically feeling up the new crime analyst who he'd found annoying mere minutes before.

He got in his car, his mind still on Mazy and his reaction to her. He hadn't dated anyone for years. The last attempt had been a nuisance. The woman was beautiful, successful, and deeply insecure. When he was too busy to text her in the day, she would blow up his phone asking if he was okay. Jackson's days were unpredictable. He didn't have the luxury of texting "sweet nothings" throughout the day. He never could determine if she just needed the attention or if she was fearful about Jackson's line of work. Regardless, Jackson had called it off and he'd been content in his single life ever since.

Mazy wasn't like that. She seemed self-assured and comfortable in who she was. She was smart, beautiful, and a little out of Jackson's league. While Jackson took good care of himself and worked out daily, he didn't consider himself a match for her in the looks department. Though he'd been told he was handsome, his face was pretty average—brown hair, hazel eyes, brown beard. Could someone like Mazy ever be attracted to someone like him?

Jackson arrived at the scene and shook his head when he spotted the yellow tape and small team of people working the scene. Nothing like a dead body to knock any attraction out of his brain.

He stood looking at the body of a man who had the same amount of bloating as Vanessa did and the same bullet wound through his forehead as Vanessa did. He felt sure his theory was correct.

"It's Eric Janson. Guarantee it," Jackson said arrogantly. He looked around. His co-workers were already leaving the scene. They'd already investigated and were packing up. They ignored him and moved away.

Jackson sighed. He guessed he'd be drinking alone tonight, again. He was well aware his co-workers thought he was a keener. Hell, they might even be right. Most nights he didn't care. But damned if he didn't feel lonely tonight.

His mind returned to Mazy. He couldn't get that smell out of his brain. It was late enough in the afternoon that he thought better of going back to the building. It would be evening soon and his only reason for going back would be to catch Mazy on her way out. No good could come from the direction of his thoughts. Better just focus on the new case.

Who in the world would kill Vanessa Ireland and Eric Allen Janson? Jackson pulled his car up to his favorite local bar.

Maybe it was murder-suicide, he thought. It was the black

plastic bag around Vanessa that made him doubt it. If the last murder victim who'd shown up wrapped like that was tied to the Deliver and Dash Killer, did it mean there was a copycat?

Jackson shivered as he took a sip of his beer. He sure hoped not.

20

JACKSON

J. Jackson cut his workout short this morning, feeling eager to get to work. He was the kind of guy who rarely strayed from his daily routine. He worked way too much, hit the bar on the way home, slept seven hours a night, woke and hit the gym before work, then finished with a hot shower. Most mornings he was at work by eight. This morning it would be earlier.

He took extra care with his appearance today. He always wore a trimmed beard. When he'd looked at himself in the mirror, he noticed his hair was getting a little long. He'd frowned at himself. He'd have to make an appointment to get a haircut soon. He put on a pair of wrangler jeans that best fit his long legs and were snug against his waist and butt. He was a fit guy, he always had been, and the business casual look only accentuated his build. He buttoned his plaid shirt and put a black corduroy jacket over it. He slipped on his most worn cowboy boots and gave himself one more glance.

"What are you doing, Jackson?" He shook his head in disgust at himself, knowing full well he was trying to impress Mazy.

Still, he walked in expecting to find the place empty. His

stomach flipped when he saw Mazy sitting at her desk. He walked up behind her quietly.

He put a hand on her shoulder. "You're here early."

Mazy screamed. "Jesus!"

"No, Jackson," he smirked as she whirled her chair around to face him. Her eyes didn't hold the same humor.

"You were right. The autopsy came back from the last Red River swimmer, and it was Eric Janson." She bit her lip. "How did you know?"

Jackson found a chair and rolled it over to her desk. He crossed his arms over his broad chest. His hazel eyes looked into her brown eyes and for a moment, he almost forgot the question.

"Oh, um, a couple years ago, we had a case—"

"Right, the Deliver and Dash murders?" she interrupted.

"Eric Janson and his girlfriend, Vanessa, were the people who'd been working at the front desk when the murderer came in to get a key. They turned off the cameras and left the key at the front desk unattended. Later, Eric admitted he owed a guy a favor and agreed to do those things. It seemed a lot like accessory to murder if you would have asked me. But Eric struck a deal to get out free. He turned in the guy—Danny Jessup, who we later found out was working with Ludwig Lacose—"

"The former lieutenant of this department," Mazy finished his sentence.

Jackson nodded. "He was the last link to Lacose who was still alive."

"I see." Mazy nodded.

"Yeah. That, and Jessup had been working with Lacose back then until he'd washed up in the Red River packaged the exact same way Vanessa washed up. He had two trash bags around his body, duct-taped together in the middle. He'd even been shot in the forehead. Every person we knew who had been working with Lacose is now dead. The prison guard who broke him out is dead. His lawyer is dead. His partner is—"

"Dead." Mazy chewed a nail. She looked young and vulnerable when she did that, but Jackson knew she was his age. She just wasn't showing it yet. He knew because he'd snooped through a personnel file. He saw the red flags on his part. But he needed to know who she was. He was attracted to her but knew nothing about her. And right now, he had no idea why Mazy looked so worried.

"Right. So, the alternative to his ghost showing up to tie up loose ends is far more terrifying."

"Copycat?" she suggested.

"Not sure," he grunted.

Jackson reluctantly broke eye contact and sat back in his chair. He put his feet up on the desk as he placed his hands behind his head and looked out the window, seeing only the building next door. He tried to think about the case, but he could only think about her. Had she come in early because she thought he'd be there? Was she thinking about him too?

"What other possibilities might we be missing?" Mazy mused.

"What if—" Jackson paused a half second. "What if there's someone out there who was part of his team? Someone we knew nothing about."

"That would be bad," Mazy acknowledged.

Jackson looked at her again and nodded slowly.

"Oh yeah," Mazy had leaned forward and was looking into his eyes. "Bad."

Something stirred in Jackson as she looked at him. Her eyes were deep and intense. Did her word have a double meaning? He took his feet off the desk and put them back on the floor, turning his whole body to face hers.

"You know, when that case was underway, I remember feeling like a failure," Jackson gulped. He'd never been so transparent before. He had no idea why he was talking to Mazy like this now. "Here we had a serial killer on the loose. We have a process and a high solve rate. But our killer was still on the street. Imagine my despair when we realized the serial killer was here in this office, right under our noses. He was someone I knew and trusted! I should have handed in my badge right then and there. I thought about it. Debated a while—"

"And then?" Mazy had moved closer.

"Then I realized the department was going to be under enough transition. They wouldn't do well to have so much turnover. But I still think about leaving. I don't have the luxury of missing such details." He held his breath a minute and exhaled loudly. "I mean, I didn't even suspect him."

"Don't leave, J," Mazy breathed.

She was now inches from him.

"You want me to stay?" he asked, closing the gap between them.

"Yes," she whispered.

"Is that all you want?" he asked.

She shook her head. It was the only invitation he needed. Jackson wheeled her chair closer so her knees snugged up against his inner thighs. He pressed his lips against hers. Her lips parted. Her mouth was warm and inviting. She tasted like coffee. Jackson kept his eyes open, watching the office door in case a co-worker decided to be early today as well.

Then he deepened the kiss, his tongue exploring the inside of her mouth. The hardness in his pants told him the kiss would not be enough. He heard sudden footsteps on the stairs. She did too and they jumped apart.

Without a word, Jackson got up and stalked to the bathroom. The bulge in his pants would be hard to explain to someone else.

Hell, it was hard for him to explain it to himself.

21

PAIGE

A bat was flying around the house. Paige was trying desperately to get the bat out of the house. She didn't think it was possible for her stomach to get any bigger, but it had. The babies were pressed against her, making it uncomfortable for her to live in her own skin. Now, out of nowhere, a bat had flown into her house.

Anna jumped up and down, not trying to help Paige out. Anna knew the bat shouldn't be in the house.

"Aww, he's a cute bat," Anna squealed in between jumps. "Don't kill it, mommy!"

Paige couldn't seem to reach the bat, let alone kill it. He definitely wasn't cute, but Paige was learning to pick and choose her battles where Anna was concerned. Anna was a very strong-willed child, and Paige didn't have as much energy to fight with her these days.

In a stroke of brilliance, Paige got a broom.

"Open the door, Anna!" Paige yelled as the broom guided the bat exactly where Paige wanted him to go—outside. After three more attempts, Paige was able to get the bat out the door without harming him, much to Anna's delight.

Paige shut the door, dropped the broom, and sank onto the couch to catch her breath. She watched Anna flap her hands as if they were wings and run around in circles.

"I want to be a bat for Halloween!" Anna declared as she flew around the living room.

Paige's cell phone rang, and she immediately answered it. She'd been keeping her phone on her these days in case James called.

"Hello?"

"Paige, it's Mona, James' mom," she greeted, her accent thick and Canadian like her son's.

"Oh, thank God! Thank you for calling me back. Have you seen James? He left for Canada three days ago. He was supposed to be back yesterday. I haven't heard from him and wondered if you had?"

The phone was silent for half a minute. When Mona did speak, it was clear she was choosing her words carefully. "Sometimes James disappears, Paige."

"I know," Paige exhaled. "I'm aware. But I don't think that's what happened this time. You know, the babies are due in less than three weeks, and he's so excited about them coming."

"James wanted to be a dad for a long time," Mona agreed quietly.

"What if something happened to him?" Paige's voice broke, and tears suddenly blinded her.

"Have you called the police services?" Mona asked.

"Yes—well, no. I called a friend of mine who works in police services, but he said the same thing you did." Paige hung her head, feeling the weight of defeat.

"Honey, if you're worried about it, call it in. Put out a missing person's request. It's the only thing you can do right now."

"Okay." Paige felt punched in the gut as she hung up the phone. She had hoped James' mother would feel the same way she did—worried about James. Weren't mothers supposed to have some intuition? Paige wouldn't know. Her mother certainly wasn't someone who had responded to things in the way "normal" mothers should.

Anna had stopped flying around and stood uncertainly in front of Paige as she cried. "It's okay, mommy." Anna crawled up on the couch beside Paige and patted her large tummy carefully.

"Thanks, Anna," Paige said as she cuddled her three-year-old, appreciating Anna's rare attempt to be comforting.

Paige's phone rang again. This time, it was a number Paige didn't recognize.

"Hello," she answered cautiously.

"Paige Friesen?" the man's voice was clipped and professional.

"Yes?" Paige's heart sped up as she immediately worried about the possibilities.

"Gilly Vance here, returning your phone call."

"Oh, Mr. Vance!" Paige sat up taller on the couch. "This is odd, but I'm looking for James Friesen. He got on a plane three days ago for a meeting at the company and he was supposed to be back yesterday, only he didn't get off the plane here. I was wondering if you saw him at all after the meeting?"

Again, Paige was greeted with silence.

Finally, Gilly answered. "Paige, you're his wife, correct?"

"Yes," she answered.

"Then I suppose it's okay to tell you that James never showed up to the meeting." Gilly delivered the news like he was firing an employee.

"He never showed up?" Paige asked, feeling dumbfounded.

"Never showed," Gilly confirmed.

"Did you report that to the police?" she asked, feeling afraid.

Gilly snorted. "No. It's not the first time James Friesen

didn't show up for a meeting. I would think you, of all people, would know what I mean by that."

Paige sighed as a new round of tears filled her eyes.

"I do," she responded sadly.

"Will there be anything else Mrs. Friesen?" he asked.

Paige shook her head. "No. Thank you." With that, she hung up the phone.

"Are you worried about Daddy James, mommy?" Anna asked.

"Yes, Anna, I'm very worried," Paige sniffled. She couldn't just sit here and do nothing. Paige took out her phone and dialed Stephen.

"Stephen, when can you be back in the area again?"

22

JACKSON

Jackson felt downright grumpy, and it had only gotten worse as the week went on. Every day since that kiss, he'd come in early, hoping to find Mazy there too. She hadn't been. When she came to work, she just showed up right on time when the station was already at a busy hustle.

Realizing he wasn't going to get a chance alone, Jackson stopped at her desk one morning and casually looked around, making sure no one was paying attention. He cursed that he hadn't paid more attention with his appearance. The thermal vest he wore over a long-sleeved t-shirt was a little worn. His hair was getting on the long side. Otherwise, he supposed he looked the same as every other day in his wranglers and cowboy boots.

He spoke in a low voice. "I've been thinking about you," he said. He cleared his voice nervously. No other woman had ever created such a response in Jackson. He didn't date much, and he'd never been married, unless he counted the job. Mazy made him nervous and excited at the same time.

"You can't think about me," she snapped. Mazy's eyes stayed on her computer screen as she pretended to keep working. This allowed him to study her. Today, she wore a tight-fitted, soft, red V-neck sweater. A dainty silver chain with a small black pearl hung at her neckline. Black pinstriped pants hugged her thin hips and fell to her ankles where she wore black high heels. Her black hair was twisted and held up by some black clip Jackson had never seen before.

"Why can't I think about you?" he asked, frustration evident in his voice.

"Because we work together," she replied. "I can't lose this job."

"No one's going to lose a job here. I just wonder if we should explore this thing."

"This thing?" her voice sounded low but sharp. Her eyes swung to his with a piercing anger Jackson did not understand. It both frightened and intrigued him.

"Mazy, I'm not very good at this—relationship things. I think it's why I'm single."

She was quiet as she went back to typing a few things on the computer screen. When Jackson didn't go away, Mazy sighed. She wrote down a name and street address on a post-it note. She handed it to Jackson.

"Why don't you meet me after work today? There's this bar where I like to stop and grab a drink on the way home," she invited him.

"Okay, great." Jackson took the note and his heart sped up as her warm fingers brushed his in the process.

Jackson leaned forward and opened his mouth to say something but shut his mouth abruptly.

"Ahem." The new Chief of Police had just walked in and eyed the pair of them with narrowed eyes. "Am I interrupting anything?"

"No," Mazy swung around to meet the chief's gaze. "Jackson was just asking for an update, and I was telling him there's no news since yesterday."

The man studied them suspiciously for a moment longer, then nodded curtly as he went into his office.

Mazy let out a sigh, gave Jackson a warning glance, and went back to her computer.

Jackson knew this was his cue to move on. But something about the ease of which her lie had rolled out of her mouth had bothered Jackson. It was so effortless, even Jackson felt compelled to believe her even though he'd experienced what had actually happened.

Was it a red flag or an excuse for him to stomp this into the ground? Jackson fingered the post-it note he'd jammed into his pocket. He continued to check for it for the better part of that day. He intended to figure out the answer tonight when he met her at the bar.

23

JAMES

When morning came and I was sure Mina was gone, I hit the floor. I'd been on my hands and knees for hours, desperately attempting to peel the baseboard away from the wall with my short fingernails. My nails were short and stubby, so I'd been unsuccessful at getting a grip on the baseboard. I knew there were thin nails holding the baseboard to the wall. I also knew they were the exact kind of nail I needed to pop open the lock on the door. So, I would keep trying until I found a weak spot.

Something had shifted with Mina. When she'd given me my breakfast this morning, it was a cold biscuit, most likely from yesterday's breakfast run. She'd set the coffee down so hard, some of it sloshed in the window slats, causing the coffee to seep down into the wood. She didn't care.

I'm a feeler. I'd learned this in rehab. Not that I'd believed it at the time. But the counselor who had helped me discover this trait was patient and helped me understand that I could feel the emotions of people around me. This had confused me for much of my life. It was hard to feel anger or hurt from another person and not take it as my own.

At first, I thought this was a huge disadvantage. In fact, I'd been so responsive and reactive to the feelings and emotions of people around me, it was hard to understand what feelings were mine and what feelings were not. Then I understood the significance of feeling the emotions of others around me. Of the ability to read the room.

This morning, I could feel that something had changed in Mina. There was a new sort of distance and determination in her demeanor. I knew what it was. It didn't matter if I had changed her mind last night, even for a minute. She was firmer and more resolved than ever before.

It's the reason I was crawling around on the floor, looking for a weak spot in the baseboards, trying to pull them away from the wall, hoping to maneuver a nail out. I didn't have time.

Mina Martin was going to kill me. And she was going to do it soon.

24

JACKSON

Mazy never showed at the bar that night. In anticipation and perhaps excitement, Jackson sipped his beer slowly. When he got his second, he realized an hour had passed and still no Mazy. He turned and let his eyes roam around the bar for the tenth time that night. He knew in his gut she wasn't coming. After another hour, Jackson realized what an idiot he'd been. He didn't even have her number. That should've told him everything he needed to know.

"You're a fool, Jackson." Jackson chastised himself as he threw cash down on the bar and walked out into the cold night alone. Though it was like every other night, spending an evening alone was the last thing Jackson wanted to do. As he went to bed that night, he put his phone on his bedstand and turned the ringer up. As a detective, he was always on call.

Am I really that bad? he thought as he drifted to sleep. No, Mazy was just really not interested. He'd get to the bottom of everything in the morning.

He was up early the next morning and made himself go through his normal routine, which seemed to take forever. Finally, Jackson made his way to the office. It was an hour earlier than his co-workers typically arrived, but he stopped short to find Mazy in the office already working. She looked sophisticated in a black turtleneck sweater that hugged her tiny frame and rounded chest. Her hair was sleek and straight, hanging to her shoulders.

Jackson walked right up to her. "Do me the favor of not inviting me out next time. I'm an adult. If you aren't interested, don't ask me out to begin with." Jackson turned to leave, feeling hurt and angry at the same time.

Mazy put her hand on his wrist, stopping his movement. "Jackson, I'm sorry. Something came up and I didn't have your number."

Jackson wanted to shake her hand off him but couldn't. Through his anger, he felt something else. That same sensation of electricity shot straight up his hand and into his heart. What was this? It was attraction to be sure. Could it be more than that? He didn't even know her.

Jackson found himself pulling closer to Mazy. He was having trouble keeping his distance. He still towered over her but now, he was close enough that his leg accidentally brushed her knee.

"Mazy, you aren't obligated to like me. You don't have to invite me out. Spare my dignity next time."

"Who said I don't like you?" Mazy said softly, her big eyes gazing up at him.

Jackson's heart dropped as he looked into her eyes. Jackson felt confused. He wanted to believe, in this moment, she did like him.

"Then why?" Jackson pushed.

Mazy stood up but barely came up to his chest in two-inch high-heeled black suede boots that stopped inches under her knee. The leather skirt she wore swung a bit as she stood. He tried not to notice her legs under that skirt were bare though it was cold outside.

"I can't get into that. I'm just asking you to trust me." Her fingers never left his wrist but now they were making soft circles on his skin.

"Mazy?" Jackson glanced nervously at the door to the office. If the boss walked in now, there would be no way to explain their close proximity.

"Hmm?" she said as she scooted even closer. It was like they were two magnets, drawn to each other, destined to be together.

"Have you ever seen the book closet?" Jackson whispered.

"The... what?" Her eyebrows furrowed quizzically.

"The book closet," Jackson murmured. He grabbed her hand and gently tugged her to a small corner office tucked away behind a closed door, taking a gamble that she would come with him. She did.

Jackson's heart beat wildly in his chest. He led Mazy into the tiny little corner office that used to be a closet but had been converted into a corner reading room lined with bookshelves full of detective stories and old literature. It smelled like old book pages when they walked in, but all Jackson could smell now was Mazy's perfume.

As they walked through the door, Mazy shut it behind them. "I didn't even know this was here."

"Yeah," Jackson said as he stared at her with intensity. He didn't have a plan exactly, just a strong desire to be alone with her.

Mazy leaned against the door and stared back at him. "Well, J. Now that you have me in here, whatever do you plan to do with me?"

It was all the invitation Jackson needed. He closed the gap between them and found her lips and covered them with his own. He was surprised with himself, but he was even more surprised when she kissed him back with equal intensity. In fact, she responded with a playful shove. The room was small, and when Jackson took a step back to catch his balance, he bumped into the window ledge and sat down hard on the window seat as Mazy advanced.

Mazy shocked him by crawling up onto his lap, cowgirl style. Her skirt fanned out beside her, leaving Jackson with the knowledge that there was very little fabric between them. Mazy kissed him roughly as her fingers laced up into his hair.

Jackson felt his pants tighten in front.

"I like your hair longer," she whispered seductively in his ear. Her warm breath sent tingles down his spine.

"I'll never cut it again," he promised. He reached under her skirt to readjust her on his lap and found a tiny string of lace holding her panties in place, otherwise, his hands held her bare bottom. The air left his body and for one minute, he wanted to tear off every piece of clothing that separated them.

Mazy began to move against his erection, slowly at first, then faster and faster. A small moan escaped her lips.

"God, Mazy. You're driving me crazy!" Jackson whispered.

"What're you gonna do about it?" she asked. She stood up and slid her panties off over her boots.

Jackson inhaled sharply.

"May I?" Mazy asked as her hands found his belt buckle. Jackson nodded, unable to speak. Mazy's hands unbuttoned his jeans and pulled down the zipper. Jackson stood as Mazy tugged at his jeans. Jackson dropped his jeans and boxers. He picked Mazy up and gently set her on the table.

"Mazy, this is where you get to tell me *no*."

Mazy lay back and crooked a finger at him.

Jackson accepted the invitation. Mazy gasped as Jackson thrust inside her, gently at first. Finding her warm and wet, Jackson picked up the speed until they were both panting and climaxing together.

It was then that Jackson heard a noise just outside the door. He froze.

Mazy must have heard it too, because she jumped up guiltily.

Jackson scrambled for his pants.

They were both breathing hard and trying to catch their breath.

"What do we do?" Mazy mouthed. She was up and looking around for her panties.

Before Jackson could answer, there was a knock at the door and the unmistakable voice of their chief called through the door. "When you two are quite finished, I would like to see you in my office."

Jackson's face showed shock and embarrassment.

"Any chance we'll just get a warning?" Mazy whispered.

"Not a chance," Jackson answered grimly.

Mazy put her hand on the doorknob, her face a bright red. Just before she opened the door, she saw the silky material of her panties peeking out from behind a bookshelf. She quickly snatched them off the floor and tucked them into her skirt pocket.

Mazy lifted her chin with false dignity, missing the way Jackson's eyes showed the laughter he dared not let out.

25

JAMES

I was lying on the floor, staring at the ceiling. I'd finally given up trying to pull the baseboard away from the wall. I'd given up altogether. My spirits were low. The kind of low that made me desperately want a drink.

Fight, James, fight, my brain tried to rally me into action.

It didn't work. I thought about Paige and tried to picture what she was doing at this very moment. Was she watching Anna play with Molly? Did she miss me? Was she worried about me? Did she think I had started drinking again? I shook my head to rid myself of that thought. Paige knew me. Surely, she was worried sick about me by now.

I refocused on a more positive thought. Had her stomach grown even bigger since I last saw her? I smiled despite myself as I thought about the night she told me she was pregnant. We were in jail, of all places. I'd willingly become an accomplice to breaking and entering into a home we thought would lead us to Anna. I would have broken into a thousand houses to find that girl.

Only, things had gone from bad to worse the minute we stepped into the house. I would never forget that stench. It was the first time I'd smelled rotten flesh and dried blood. Then we'd found the source. Two people had been murdered in that living room, then moved. There was an actual earlobe laying on the living room floor.

Then, the owner came home. Demitri Abbott was a pure psychopath. While Paige and I hid out in the water heater closet, we listened, unable to stop the man, as he murdered someone else. I called 911, but it didn't matter. When they found us in the closet in the same room with a gun, they had no choice but to throw us in jail.

It was sheer luck and a good lawyer that got us out of that one. Had I really come so far, overcome so many odds, just to die here now? Paige was due to pick me up from the airport. Was that supposed to happen today? I had no idea how many days had gone since I'd been taken.

I pictured her in labor, remembering she'd shared how alone she'd felt when she had Anna. It was only her in that delivery room. I had promised Paige she would never be alone again.

Angrily, I kicked the wall. The flat part of my boot connected with the wall hard. I was wearing the kind of lace up construction boot that had a steel toe and hard, durable soles.

I heard the noise instantly. The noise of hope. It was the sound of a crack. Like wood splintering from the wall. Dare I look? I peeked at the wall to see I had, indeed, cracked the baseboard.

I kicked it again and again, too many times to count. The baseboard broke and I sat up. I grabbed a broken piece and pulled it from the wall. Tears of joy filled my eyes. I could see nails.

Now I just needed a way to get the nail out of the baseboard. I needed to do it fast. The clock was ticking.

26

JACKSON

Jackson hunched his shoulders against the cold. He'd lived in Canada his whole life, but the cold never bothered him until today. He'd never lost a job before today either. Certainly not for such an idiotic reason. His mind went to Mazy as the new chief scolded them like second graders. It was clear from Mazy's white face that she had never lost a job for this reason either.

The chief had looked up and spotted them in the window on his way in. By the time Jackson and Mazy had collected themselves and made it to the office, the chief's face was a purple color.

"The workplace is not appropriate for such things," he had said in a low growl.

Jackson supposed he could have argued they weren't technically doing *such things* during work hours. Instead, he'd wisely kept his mouth shut. He had no longevity with the new chief, and a part of him felt like he'd lost his edge during the Deliver and Dash case. He didn't have the energy to argue to try and keep the job.

Jackson had quietly gathered what little he had in his locker and left. He supposed after ten years in the force, it was sad he only kept a change of clothes in a gym bag and a picture of the day he'd started as a rookie.

He thought about waiting for Mazy, who'd been asked to stay behind, but he decided to give her space. Instead, he threw his work odds and ends into his car and drove to a breakfast diner around the corner from his house.

He thought about going to the bar—he knew of one that was open at this time of morning from his beat days. Cops needed a place to go after they got off shift to drink and decompress from working overnight shifts. It was the same neighborhood bar he'd always gone to. He thought about going there. Only, he didn't feel like drinking.

Instead, he chose the diner. He was on his second cup of coffee when Mazy walked in. He turned and felt his eyes light up when she walked through the door. He couldn't help it. Stupid or not, he didn't regret what little time he'd spent with her.

Mazy's eyes widened and she backed out the same door she'd just come in.

"Mazy, wait," Jackson called. He turned to the waitress, "I'll be right back."

She was already walking quickly down the street, he guessed to her car. Clearly, she didn't want to see him.

"Mazy, please. Will you just talk to me?" Jackson ran after her.

Mazy halted and stood right where she was as he approached. He would've admired her backend and legs in that skirt, but he just thought she looked cold. She turned slowly, revealing the black smudges of mascara staining her cheeks.

"I'm sorry," Jackson said as he softly touched her arm. He looked her in the eyes. "I knew better. I'm sorry."

"I see," she said coldly. "You knew better than I did? Why? Because you're the guy?"

Despite the cold, Jackson's face reddened. "I didn't mean that."

"He asked me if I had felt pressured into that." Mazy swiped at a new set of tears. Her hand shook. "It was so humiliating!"

"God!" Jackson was suddenly horrified over the implications of her words. He wanted to ask her how she'd answered. But he didn't want to make this about him.

"I'm not sure if you've noticed, but I do what I want, when I want, with whom I want. Damn the consequences. Apparently," she spat out strongly.

"Okay, fine." Jackson put his shoulders back. "I'm not sorry then."

Confusion entered Mazy's eyes. "You're not?"

Jackson shook his head. "I'd choose to get fired from every job just to be with you over and over again."

Mazy smirked but looked unconvinced. "That was… embarrassing," she whispered. Tears temporarily clouded her vision.

"Yeah," Jackson agreed as he scratched the back of his head. "You look like you're freezing," he said as he held his hands out. "You're shaking. Come here."

Cautiously, she took a step forward and Jackson opened his jacket and folded her into it as he put his arms around her. They huddled there for body heat for a minute. Jackson put his chin down and rested it on the top of her head. Her hair smelled like some floral arrangement, and he felt instantly intoxicated.

"Mazy, can I buy you breakfast? We've had a helluva day already," Jackson said. To his surprise, she giggled.

She ran her hands down his spine as she looked up at him. "Yeah," she agreed.

They walked back into the diner and sat in the warmth until a cheerful server approached them. She refilled the coffee cup Jackson had left behind. She brought a cup for Mazy. They ordered breakfast.

"Jackson isn't your first name. Neither is J," Mazy looked at him sheepishly. "I should probably know your first name. It was like the best kept office secret."

Jackson shuddered. "I pity the person who let that cat out. I might have paid the first human resources person to *not* put my first name on anything. It's awful and if I tell you, you must take the secret to your grave."

Mazy sat up straighter and tried to look serious, but gazing into Jackson's serious eyes made her giggle unexpectedly. "I promise."

"It's Jarrold," he said in a low, almost imperceptible voice.

Mazy leaned forward and cuffed her hand behind her ear. "What, I can't hear you?"

Jackson was off his chair in one quick motion, and he sat down next to her. He scooted his chair close to her, looked into her eyes, and tucked a strand of silky, black hair behind her ear. He leaned close and whispered his name in her ear.

Mazy shivered.

Jackson sat up straight again. "If you ever tell anyone, I'll deny it."

Mazy giggled again and turned toward the steaming eggs and fluffy pancakes that now sat in front of them. Breakfast had been served without their knowledge. They continued to talk about things like favorite childhood memories. The moment when Jackson decided to become a cop and then a detective and how hard the training had been.

Jackson told Mazy about his family—one brother and two overbearing parents who stayed together though they really shouldn't have. Mazy told Jackson she was an only child, and her parents were long gone.

Breakfast turned into lunch. They stayed so long they ordered a second meal. It wasn't lost on them that this might have to be their last meal out until they found other jobs. But it was also becoming clear they didn't want to leave each other. Not to mention, they had nowhere else to go.

"You know the worst thing about losing a job?" Mazy asked as she sipped her coffee. She pushed a finger into the hamburger bun. She was just playing with her food now.

"Tell me," Jackson commanded gently.

"I've never lost a job before. It's the one thing I could always brag about."

"Oh, come on," Jackson teased with a small smile. "There has to be more claim to fame than that!"

Mazy looked at her half-eaten plate of food. "Jackson, I…" she looked at him like she was going to tell him something but changed her mind. "I was a poor kid growing up—"

"Same," Jackson said. He put his hand on the table between her and him. He wanted to reach out to her, but he wanted her to meet him halfway.

Mazy sat up taller and leaned her head to the side, looking sideways at him with her fist under her chin. "I mean, it was so bad for me. I ran away before I finished high school. I don't actually have a diploma."

"Wow!" Jackson felt impressed. "You've done well for yourself, eh?"

Mazy shrugged. "I don't actually tell people that."

"How'd you get the job at police services?" he wondered.

"I lied. Just like I have on every other job application and on resumes I turn in. I have the qualifications and I'm damn smart—"

"I'll say!" Jackson snorted. Something about this survival technique tickled him. "You lied your way into a police services job, and no one was the wiser?"

"That's not admirable, Jackson." Mazy looked dejected. "I've done a lot of things I'm not proud of to survive the streets. Or get off them."

"I bet," Jackson looked serious again. "I just cost you a job that was important to you and keeping you off the streets."

Mazy shook her head. "I cost myself. I knew I needed to stay away from you."

"Why? Why am I so bad for you?" Jackson protested. His hand still rested between them.

Mazy grabbed his hand. Jackson sucked in air. "Just so you know, I feel it too, J. There's this electrical current between us. You didn't even like me in the beginning, but you couldn't hide your attraction to me."

"I'll say," Jackson agreed. He was looking into her eyes, beyond the smudged makeup, and he felt captivated by something much deeper. He would be an idiot to let her walk out of here without him. That would end the spell.

"You admit you didn't like me?" Mazy sounded outraged and amused simultaneously now.

"Absolutely!" Jackson admitted with a smug grin. "It wasn't you though. I just really missed your predecessor. She was a helluva crime analyst. She's the one who created the system we follow—*followed* when we worked there—to keep moving toward the goal to solve crimes as fast and accurately as possible."

"Mina? That was her name, right?" Mazy asked.

"Yes," Jackson agreed.

"Did you ask her to the book closet too?" Mazy winked at him as she tapped his shoulder with hers.

"God, no!" Jackson pulled back, horrified. "I've never done that before in my life. Not at work."

"Why me?" she asked. She moved closer, closing the gap.

Jackson met her and they were inches from each other, still holding hands. "Because you're smart and beautiful. And every time I smell your hair or perfume, I lose my mind a bit. Then I started picturing a life with you. I don't know you that well, but something about you makes me want to spend a lifetime fixing that. Jesus, I've really not done this in a long time. Am I supposed to be this honest?"

"It's really working for me, J," her voice was husky and breathless at the same time.

"What now?" Jackson asked.

"I say we finish what we started," Mazy said. "Turns out, I've got the day off and so do you."

"Yeah, I agree. My place is right around the corner," Jackson said as he opened his wallet and threw money on the table.

The waitress was there then, scooping their food into to-go containers. They grabbed them mindlessly, not thinking about the fact that money would run out without jobs. They didn't care about that right now.

They made it to Jackson's apartment, but neither of them remembered the drive over. They'd barely shut the door when Mazy pushed Jackson against the door. He put his hand gently behind her neck and leaned down. His lips found hers and for minutes, they kissed. Finally breathless, Mazy took a half step back.

"May I?" Mazy asked as she reached to unbutton his jeans.

"Allow me," he responded. He unbuckled his belt.

Mazy's hands unbuttoned his jeans as he started kissing her again. He pushed his jeans down over his hips, and they fell to the ground with a clanking sound. Jackson shrugged out of his coat and took off his shirt.

Mazy groaned as her hands moved over his flat stomach and defined abs. Her light touch tickled him. He pushed her hands away to unzip her skirt, which fell effortlessly to the ground. Next, he pulled off her turtleneck sweater. She was wearing matching black bra and panties. She still wore the knee-high boots. She made a move to remove them, but he stopped her.

"Leave them," he requested. Before she could answer, he picked up her petite frame and shoved her against the wall. She wrapped her legs around him. Jackson took a deep breath to calm himself. It had been too long since he'd had this kind of chemistry with a woman. Mazy gasped as she began to move against him. This was going to undo him. Jackson turned and sat her on the couch. He kicked off his boots, took off his boxers, and looked her in the eyes.

"Good Lord," she murmured. "Size is not a problem with you, is it, J?" Mazy moved to put her mouth on him.

"Wait," he commanded gently. He kneeled in front of her instead. She lifted her bottom as he removed her panties. "You first."

Mazy gasped as Jackson made his way to the place where her panties had warmed her minutes before. She felt his wet tongue pleasure her and she let her eyes close as she enjoyed the moment. Then his fingers slipped inside her and Mazy began to climax loudly. When she finished, she opened her eyes to see Jackson looking pretty proud of himself.

Mazy got up and pushed Jackson to a sitting position. She promptly climbed onto his lap and fit him inside her. She pumped herself repeatedly up and down over his erection, faster and faster until he could no longer contain himself. At the moment that he lost it, Mazy climaxed again and for minutes, they sat still in that position, afraid to move or breathe.

"Holy shit," Jackson said breathlessly.

"Exactly," Mazy agreed.

Then they fell asleep tangled in each other's arms right there on the couch. Jackson had thought about her for weeks and knew it would be amazing. He had no idea how much better the real thing would be. As he drifted to sleep with her in his arms, he realized he would be an idiot to ever let her go.

27

PAIGE

"Mommy's going on a trip!" Anna announced when Stephen walked through the door that afternoon. Paige had gotten lucky. Stephen was in the area and between cases, which meant he could keep Anna for a while.

"Oh, she is, is she?" Stephen's eyes watched Paige's movements.

Paige moved quickly, frantically, as she darted from the living room and back into her bedroom where there was a suitcase opened on her bed.

"Where are you going, Paige?" Stephen had followed her to the doorway of her bedroom with a concerned look on his face.

"Boundaries, Stephen," Paige snapped.

Stephen held his hands up as he leaned against the door frame. It was not lost on him that he'd been lying right where he was standing in a pool of his own blood many years ago.

"What are you doing, Paige?" he asked.

Paige stopped and looked at him for a moment. All the worry and fear broke as tears flooded her eyes then fell in torrents down her cheeks.

"What happened?" he asked.

"I called—" her voice broke. "No one has seen James. Not his mom. Not his boss. He didn't even show up to the meeting—"

"He didn't show up to the meeting he went to Canada for?" Now Stephen looked concerned. Paige shook her head. "Think back, Paige. The last conversation you had with James. How did he sound?"

"Happy." Paige wiped her face and sniffed. "He'd just gotten off the plane. He talked to me, and he talked to Anna. Then he let me go because his ride was there."

"His ride?" Stephen asked. "His ride to take him where?"

"To the work meeting. He was selling his company. He was coming back home in two days," Paige said. Her voice sounded whiny.

"Did he say who picked him up?" Stephen asked.

Paige shook her head. "I didn't even think to ask. He just said, *Gotta go, my ride is here. I'll call you later tonight.*"

"Who told you he never showed up to the meeting?" Stephen asked.

"Gilly Vance, the CEO of the company," Paige answered.

"You trust him?" Stephen asked professionally. He had snapped back into cop mode.

"I don't know, Stephen!" Paige threw her hands up. "Why would he lie?"

"Not sure," Stephen responded. "But someone is lying. Who knew James was coming?"

"His boss, the people he was meeting, anyone from the office who helped organize it, I guess. He'd told his mom. He was planning to pop by and say *hello* before he came back home. That's it, that's all I know." Paige swiped impatiently at a tell-tale tear.

"Do you have Gilly's number?" Stephen asked.

Paige looked down at her phone. "Yes, he just called me earlier."

"Okay, can you send that number to me? I'd like to hear the roster of people who knew James was coming. We can start there. Typically, if work sends a car to pick up from the airport, it's to ensure the VIP gets to the destination. I'm curious where that car went if it didn't go to the office. I bet Gilly Vance has the answers to those questions."

"But he said—"

"Paige, you should know better than anyone, the bad guy isn't gonna call you up and confess. Especially if he's hiding your husband." Stephen held up a hand to cut her off. "And I'm not saying he's a bad guy. I'm still not convinced this isn't just another one of those episodes James has…"

Paige folded her arms obstinately over her bulging belly. "Judge away, Stephen."

"Daddy?" Anna's voice sounded behind him. "Are we going soon?"

"We are," Stephen said, "but mommy isn't going anywhere. Stop packing, Paige. You know you can't fly when you're this far along. You told me that yourself. Doctor's orders. But do send me Gilly's number. I'll make a phone call, Paige. Just don't get your hopes up."

That's all I need, Paige thought, *Stephen calling the shots again…*

"Tell mommy bye, Anna." Stephen patted Anna's back.

"Bye, mommy!" Anna said with a burst of energy and ran back to give Paige a hug.

Stephen turned, took Anna's hand, and Paige listened as they walked out the door. After a few minutes, she heard the car start, back out of the gravel driveway, and drive away.

Relishing the quiet, Paige sank onto the bed and closed her eyes. She felt like she was finally drifting peacefully away. With Anna's nightmares, it had been so long since she last slept well.

After what must have been hours, Paige's cell began to ring. So deep was her sleep, she couldn't seem to wake up. She blinked, not quite understanding what made her wake up. Then she heard her cell phone ring again. She gasped awake. She picked the phone up off her bed and looked at the screen. Her eyes bulged. Surely, she must be dreaming right now.

The name on her ringing screen showed the words *Hubby James*.

28

JACKSON

"Mazy, we have to go out," Jackson had announced that afternoon.

"Why?" Mazy asked. She readjusted the blanket and cuddled closer to Jackson. They had spent the last three days watching TV, cuddling on the couch, making love, sleeping, and then repeating the whole routine.

"Because we can't isolate in my apartment forever."

"I think we can," Mazy smiled flirtatiously and made a move to lift his shirt.

"Come on," Jackson coaxed. "I'm stir-crazy and we could use some food and beer."

"Oh." Mazy sat up. "That does sound important."

That's what had landed them at the bar. For the past few hours, Jackson had been chatting with the bartender and an old friend of his who sat next to him at the bar.

Having just finished a plate of nachos, Jackson noticed Mazy sipping her beer quietly. He leaned over. "Are you okay?"

She smiled and nodded. "I'm not one to get falling-down drunk," she explained. "I'd rather not ever get drunk at all, actually."

"How come?" he asked.

"I don't like feeling out of control. I'm content to relax with one beer, two at the most."

Jackson was quite the opposite. "Hope you don't mind if I do—get drunk and out of control?"

Mazy smiled and patted his hand. Jackson took that as consent. Near the fifth round, Jackson made a surprising career announcement. He stood up, surprised to find himself still sober and quite of sound mind.

"Hey, everyone!" he yelled. Mazy looked at him in surprise. The bar got momentarily quiet. "I'm gonna be a private investigator. I'm opening a firm. Let me know if you need to find anything that the police are too busy to find."

"Hooray!" Someone in the back shouted. Then the whole bar erupted in pandemonium.

Mazy laughed in genuine surprise.

Jackson sat back down. He might have underestimated how much he had drunk. In this moment, he didn't care. He sat back down and pulled Mazy close to him. She tipped her head up with laughter in her eyes. With no thought, he kissed her, softly at first and then with more passion.

"J," she pulled away hesitantly.

"You're right, you're right," he said merrily. "We're in public. I want you to be my personal crime analyst."

"Mixing business and personal?" she asked wearily. She pushed back from his arms. "I don't know if that's a good idea, J."

"It's a great idea!" he said with excitement. "Best idea of the day!"

Mazy shrugged.

Jackson peered at her more closely. "You know, you remind me of someone."

Mazy laughed lightly but looked uncomfortable. "Cut it out, J."

"No really. You are so similar to..." He moved his face closer to hers and looked like he might kiss her again. "You have the same mannerisms as..." he frowned and looked puzzled, like he was working to solve the case of the century.

"I gotta go, J," Mazy said suddenly.

"Wait," he howled. "Mazy, where you goin' eh?"

Mazy got up and walked out of the bar.

"I'm sorry," he called after her. "You don't have to work for me. You can be my partner."

Mazy walked back to him and stood in front of him. She waved a hand over him. "This—tonight—has just been too much."

"I'm sorry," Jackson said immediately. He didn't feel sorry though. He felt excited. "I don't want to lose you."

"You're not," Mazy said quietly. She hugged him. "I just need a little time to myself. Okay?"

"You sure?" Jackson asked, feeling crushed.

"Yeah, I'll be back," Mazy promised. She kissed him softly.

Before Mazy turned, Jackson thought he saw something new in her eyes. What was it? It was an emotion he'd never seen on her before—fear.

He watched as the beautiful Mazy walked away from him. *There goes your crime analyst,* his mind taunted him. He got up clumsily and followed her outside.

"Does this mean you're turning down the job?" he called after her in a joke.

Mazy's laugh echoed through the parking lot, but she didn't stop walking. He watched her pause as an Uber pulled into the parking lot. If he hadn't been so drunk, it would have occurred to him that Mazy must have called that Uber a while ago.

As he watched her, Jackson saw her take out her phone. She put it up to her ear and he saw the way the light from the screen illuminated her face. For half a second, she looked angry.

Her eyes darkened and everything pleasant about her features fell. Her countenance seemed suddenly dark.

Jackson shook his head as he turned to go back inside. He looked over his shoulder to make sure Mazy got in the Uber.

Mazy was now sitting in the car with the door still opened and one hand paused on the door handle. The phone was pressed against her ear. She was glaring right at him.

Jackson hadn't meant to meet her eyes but shivered involuntarily. That shiver was not from the cold. He half-heartedly raised a hand then went in the bar. He immediately paid his tab and called his own Uber.

"Maybe I should quit drinking," he mumbled to himself, feeling a little spooked.

29

JAMES

It had taken me hours to finagle a nail out of the baseboard. I'd tried hitting it against the floor to reverse engineer it out of the board. I'd tried pulling it out with my fingernails. I had broken one fingernail down to the quick in the process, which made me howl out loud. Then I sucked the blood that rose to the surface.

Finally, some time into the afternoon, I'd gotten the nail out only to find I'd misjudged the size. Though the nail was small, it didn't pop the lock the way I'd thought it would.

I was so intent on trying to make the nail fit that I'd missed Mina coming home. It wouldn't have mattered except Mina chose that moment to throw open the door to the room. It was as if she'd known exactly what I was doing.

The door yanked open, pulling me forward and knocking me off balance. The nail I'd been using went flying. Before I could comprehend that the door was opened, Mina shoved me hard. I took several steps backwards, almost fell, and stood wobbling for half a minute before my view landed on a terrifying site. Mina was in front of me holding a gun.

"No funny business," Mina said as she placed a gun to my forehead. She'd come home early. Or was it the same as every other day? Only, she'd come right into my room. If I would have had my wits about me, I might have rushed the door. There was no phone or window to indicate what time it was. In fact, the only way I had any inkling of time was when Mina was home for lunch or was off work.

I was fixated on the gun she held in her hand.

Did she really believe I couldn't overpower her? In heels, Mina didn't quite hit five feet tall. Still, I had to remind myself that she had managed to kidnap me despite our physical differences. But I knew she was perfectly capable of shooting a gun to kill me. I could not underestimate her.

"What are you doing?" I asked cautiously as I backed up until I hit the wall, well aware she could shoot me right here, right now if she chose.

"You are calling your wife," Mina announced. She was holding my cell phone in her hand.

"You're letting me go. Thank God—" I said, feeling my shoulders sag with relief.

"Quite the opposite," Mina interrupted rudely as she put my phone up to my face. I watched facial recognition unlock the phone. "You are going to call Paige and tell her three things and only three things."

"Okay," I said slowly. "What three things, eh?"

"You have been kidnapped. You are in Winnipeg. You will tell her where to find you after she arrives in town. No mention of me. Don't give any clues, or…" Mina waved the gun around. I ducked, knowing full well she had bullets in that chamber. Her finger hovered around the trigger. Had she been trained on how to use that thing? Certainly, no one had ever taught her to keep her finger off the trigger. That, or she didn't care if it accidentally went off.

"Okay," I agreed wisely, knowing it was the only possible course of action.

"It will be a slightly less effective revenge if I shoot you while you're on the phone with her, but I will if I must. At least she will still hear you cry out."

I sucked in air. "I believe you."

"Good. Now tell it to call your wife." Mina held up my phone again.

"Call wifey phone," I commanded Siri.

We listened to it ring on speaker phone. Then, Mina pointed the phone at me and hit the FaceTime button.

"James. Oh my God. James. Are you okay? Where are you?" Paige's frantic voice sounded shrieky and her face filled the screen.

"I've been kidnapped," I said immediately. My eyes flicked to Mina. She nodded and made a gesture that told me to continue.

"What?" Paige asked in surprise. "I knew it! Who has you? Why?" Her face looked swollen and puffy like she'd been crying. I also had to consider she might be swelling more as she neared the end of her pregnancy. At the thought, my pulse sped up. Would I make it home to see her and the babies? Would I ever make it home?

"I've been kidnapped," I repeated mechanically.

"By who? Where are you?" she asked again. I could hear the panic in her voice.

"I *mean, eh*… I can tell you I'm in Winnipeg," I said, choosing my words carefully.

"Where in Winnipeg?" she asked. "Is someone there with you now?"

"You just need to come here, Paige. I *mean, eh*… I can tell you where I am when you get here."

"You want me to get on a plane?" Paige asked suspiciously, disbelief evident in her voice. "Now?"

"I've been kidnapped. I'm in Winnipeg. I *mean, eh*… I need you to come here." I repeated the three things just as Mina instructed. I watched Mina nod in approval. She made a cut signal at her throat and abruptly hung up the phone.

"Good job, James. You get to live another day." Mina kept the gun on me as she backed out of the door and shut it behind her.

Before Mina could turn the lock, I rushed the door. I put all my weight into it. I threw the door open so quickly and with so much force, the door hit Mina. Mina, clearly caught off guard, went flying backwards. Her gun flew out of her hand. I could hear the steel of the Glock hit the floor once, bounce, and hit the ground again, sliding across the floor.

I didn't go for the gun. I didn't stop to assess the situation. I just ran. I unlocked the front door. I had it opened and was one foot out the door before I caught movement from the stunned Mina out of my peripheral.

I hadn't bought myself much time, so I sprinted. I was a runner. I assumed Mina was not. *That should give me the upper hand.* Not to mention those high-heeled boots she wore.

I hadn't expected the door to lead to a parking garage. Weren't we in an apartment building? It was as if this apartment was isolated on the lower level of a parking garage. Ground level. That would help me here.

I sprinted through rows of cars, through the parking garage, to where the parking garage ended. I ran out of the parking lot entrance which led to a small clearing and then a cluster of trees. The trees were sparse and had no leaf cover. I paused to consider for one moment. Forward or backward. Those were my only choices.

I looked back. That pause had cost me. I saw Mina holding the gun. As I turned to run, I realized I was too late. My brain registered the sound of the gun. It echoed through the parking garage. Everything moved in slow motion. I imagined the bullet making a whizzing sound as it traveled as fast as the speed of light.

Pain ripped into my shoulder. The force threw me forward. I saw the cold ground rising up to hit me as my knees buckled.

The searing agony took my breath away. I was going to die. I could hear her methodical heels clicking against the concrete floor. She was coming closer. Walking with deliberate, slow steps.

Fight, James, fight. Die fighting right here and now, my brain screamed at me. Miraculously, my body allowed me to stand. *Run, James! Ignore the pain!*

I knew better. But I also knew this was my only chance. I hadn't made it far enough from the apartment to have put enough distance between me and Mina.

I heard her laugh echoing around me.

"Did you really think you'd get far, James?" Mina called out.

Fighting the dizziness and ignoring the warning signals in my body to stop moving, I started running again. I felt a shot of adrenaline, and I pushed myself and my body. I could feel bare tree branches hitting my face and whipping my body as I ran, stumbling blindly.

I was doing okay until a branch hit me with unbudgeable force squarely on the shoulder the bullet had punctured.

Then everything went black. With some relief, I surrendered myself to the blackness where I would feel no more pain.

30

PAIGE

Paige stood staring at the phone in shock. She'd immediately called Stephen. Stephen had ended his afternoon activities with Anna, loaded her into the car, and had come back to the house.

"Paige." Stephen had come into the room and gently taken the phone from her hand. Paige jumped to attention. It was like she'd forgotten Stephen was on his way.

Stephen looked at her phone. After pushing a few buttons, Stephen grumbled to himself more than to Paige. "Don't you have a location tracker? Everyone does these days…"

"His location settings are turned off," Paige answered quickly. "You believe me now."

"Yeah, of course," Stephen said, still messing with Paige's phone.

"Can you help?" she asked, feeling helpless. "Should I call the police?"

"Paige, I might be able to help. Just remember I'm new on the job. I'll need to get clearance but since I'm a US Marshal, I know I can cross state lines. I know I have jurisdiction in Canada. I just need permission to go. To get permission, I need just cause. If we really believe James is kidnapped in Winnipeg, I could go poke around but you need to report him missing first. Can you call someone you know? Someone you trust?"

Paige nodded and took the phone back. She dialed Jackson's cell number. The phone rang three times before he answered.

"Hello?" Jackson's voice was groggy.

Paige paused. *Is he still sleeping in the afternoon?* "Jackson, it's Paige."

"Hey," he answered. "You find James yet?"

"That's why I'm calling. He just called me. He said he's been kidnapped and he's still in Winnipeg. I need to put in an official missing person's report."

"Sorry, Paige, I can't help you with that."

"What? Why?" Paige felt so devastated in that moment, she began to cry. Every time she made headway with one person, she had a setback with another. Tears spilled down her cheek for what seemed like the hundredth time that week. "I just want to find my husband!"

"I don't exactly work for the police service anymore. I got fired," Jackson said.

Paige gasped and only cried harder.

"Shit, Paige. Don't cry. I'm starting a PI business, *apparently*," Jackson said, his voice laced with sarcasm. "Are you coming up to Winnipeg?"

"I think I don't have a choice," Paige sniffed. "James said I need to come."

Stephen gently finagled the phone from Paige's tight grip and put the phone on speaker. "Hey, this is US Marshal Stephen Wilton. I'm a friend of Paige's. I was in the area when she got the phone call from James. She can't get on a plane right now, Jackson. She is eight-and-a-half months pregnant. She's not supposed to fly."

"US Marshal, you say?" Jackson asked. "You're the guy who came up here when we took down Lacose! The ex-boyfriend."

"Yeah. Listen, Paige remembers James telling her his ride was picking him up from the airport and escorting him to the meeting when he first landed. Only, his boss says James never showed up to the meeting. Is there any way you can get footage from in the airport to see who intercepted James there?"

"Sure. At least, I could have two days ago. But as I was telling Paige, I don't work for the police services anymore. I don't even have my business license yet for my PI firm."

"Okay, hang tight," Stephen commanded. "I'm on my way. Will you meet me in Winnipeg when I get there? I might need your help with this."

"Yeah, I'll stand by. But you really do need to call it in to police services."

"Will do," Stephen agreed. He hung up the phone. He turned to Paige. "I need to run this by my deputy director. But you stay put. I'll go up and try to find James. Don't worry, Paige. We'll bring him back."

Paige nodded soundlessly.

Stephen turned back to Paige. "I'll need to call Gilly Vance, too, to see who knew James was coming to Canada."

Feeling in a state of shock, Paige tuned Stephen out as he told Anna he wouldn't be taking her, and mommy wasn't going on a trip after all. She could hear Anna wail as Stephen said *goodbye*. But Paige's mind was hundreds of miles away. It was in Winnipeg, Canada.

Paige dialed the number to the Police Service of Winnipeg, her hands shaking. She could hear the way her voice wobbled as she put in an official missing person's report for her husband, James Friesen. Relaying the information seemed so final. Like she was admitting defeat.

She tried not to remember the last time she trusted a higher-up in the police services there. She shuddered. That had changed the entire course of her life. And here she was again. She hung up the phone after hearing the assurances that they would call her with any news once they'd investigated.

She wasn't so sure of the competencies of the police services there, or if she could trust them, but she was sure of Stephen's ability to bring James back. She just hoped Stephen wouldn't be bringing him back in a body bag.

31

STEPHEN

Deputy Director Rob was surprisingly easy to work with, a fact Stephen felt grateful for. He was fine with Stephen traveling to Canada to pursue the kidnapping.

"It's a perk of the job, Stephen. We work hard solving cases. We're at a stand-still with the Abbot case. We've had no movement or leads for a while. We don't have anything else pressing right now—no big cases we're working here. Obviously, I'll call you back if anything comes up. But for now, I can loan you out to find your friend. Go be a hero!" Rob had stated jovially.

Stephen knew he'd gotten lucky, and it was only a matter of time before a new case would open up. Then, his window of time would close. He needed to act quickly.

Gilly Vance, the CEO of James' company in Canada, was not as easy to work with, as it turned out.

"US Marshal, eh?" Gilly Vance had barked into the phone when Stephen finally got through to him. That had been an ordeal as well. It had taken several transfers and several polite requests to *Hold, please* before Stephen finally got through.

"Yes, I'm US Marshal Stephen Wilton. I'm calling to request

a list of names of people who knew James Friesen was coming in for that meeting."

"What's this about?" Gilly asked sharply. "I already talked to his wife. You might as well know this as well. James has a tendency to disappear, if you know what I mean—"

"I do actually know what you mean, Gilly. I'm well aware of his tendencies. Unfortunately, in this case, we have reason to suspect that James has been kidnapped—"

"Kidnapped?" Gilly interrupted in shock and horror.

"Yes, but I cannot get into the particulars of this case. I can subpoena the information we need, but as time is of the essence, I thought I would just ask if you would supply the list. You and James are on good terms, I assume?" Stephen asked knowing even if they were not, Gilly would swear they were. Gilly would think it would clear him off the suspect list faster. However, Stephen would not be crossing Gilly's name off *any* list any time soon.

"Of course, James and I are on good terms. It's just that this deal—this takeover—was confidential. Surely you understand that until papers are signed, we cannot let news of possible ownership transfer leak out. It would be detrimental. It would—"

"Gilly, with all due respect, I'm from the States. I don't know anyone in Canada. My only agenda here is to find James Friesen. I'm working in conjunction with the police services, and they can get a warrant for the information. Again, my bigger concern here is that James might not have that much time." Stephen picked up a pen and poised it over paper as he heard the impossible man sigh deeply and pause for thirty seconds.

"As I said, this information is highly confidential. If it is misused in any way, I will be forced to sue. And don't think I won't sue the police services either."

Stephen rolled his eyes but summoned a patient voice. "You have my word."

"Okay," Gilly stated with a slightly lowered voice. "Marilyn Cho, Michael Sampson, Peter Smith, Latoya Johnson, and me. I assume you'll want their contact numbers?"

"Yes, please." Stephen felt relieved. "Are they all from Canada?"

"Marilyn and Peter are. Michael is from New York. Latoya is from LA. They are executives from the same company in different offices with plans to rebrand this company and merge it with theirs," Gilly informed Stephen with an air of importance.

Stephen didn't tell him it sounded like Gilly was about to be out of a job, though he would have loved to. Instead, Stephen thanked Gilly and hung up the phone. He would have preferred to question each person face to face but maybe he could get Michael and Latoya on a Zoom call so he could look them in the eye. He'd plan to meet Peter and Marilyn when he got to Canada.

Stephen thought of Paige in tears with her protruding pregnant stomach and knew he would not come home from Canada until he had her husband in tow. He told himself it was for Anna. Anna needed her mother to be happy. But Stephen knew, deep down, he was the one who needed to see Paige happy.

32

MINA

When James threw back that door, not only did Mina go flying, but she lay there a minute or two, experiencing pain in her hip and right side of her body where she had hit the ground. She lay there feeling stunned just long enough to buy James time. Her gun had flown out of her hand. Everything seemed to slow down. Mina knew once James got away, she'd never see him again.

"No!" she yelled. She'd worked too hard to exact her revenge. She wouldn't stop now.

Get up! Lacose's voice was low and furious in her ear. *He's getting away!*

Mina obeyed. She rolled over, pushed up to her knees, then to her feet, and ran to grab the gun. The door was still wide open, and she ran through it.

She remembered the cameras just in time. She casually hid the gun behind her back and angled her body in a discreet way, knowing exactly where the cameras were positioned.

She'd used her computer tech background knowledge to disable the cameras when she was in the planning phase of kidnapping James. But then she noticed the building crew out inspecting them the next day. That was the last thing she needed. Them, asking questions.

She knew this lower level was overflow parking for residents who owned more than one car. They paid extra for their spot and the cameras were there to ensure no one messed with the cars. After that fail, Mina had enabled the cameras.

Mina was past the camera sights now and jogging. She was still trying to appear casual. Then she caught movement. She must not have been down that long, because she could see James sprint out of the parking lot and run toward the woods. At his pace, she would never catch him.

She needed to act fast. Still mindful of the cameras, she ducked behind a parked truck in the parking garage that most likely belonged to someone who lived upstairs. She could see the trees just beyond the garage and angled her gun. She had always hit her target when she practiced with her co-workers at the police services. She aimed for James' back before he could fully disappear into the woods.

She had a slight disadvantage because the sun had started to set. It was getting darker outside. But when she pulled the trigger, she hit him. She watched with satisfaction as James' body stopped abruptly and jerked forward. Relief flooded her. Her arrogance returned. She got up, casually moved the gun behind her back, and walked forward one step at a time while scanning her surroundings.

She watched as James stumbled a step, then landed on his knees.

"Did you really think you'd get that far?" she reacted with a heartless laugh.

But then he got up! She could hear his body noisily hitting tree branches as he moved deeper into the sparse wooded area.

"James, where are you going?" Mina quietly sang out. "I can see you, you know. You won't get away from me."

But Mina paused, feeling concerned. She had been bluffing.

While it was true there were no leaves on the trees, and she could see well enough, it was getting darker by the minute. James was moving fast again. Where had she hit him? It was only a matter of time before he slowed down and hit the ground again. Wasn't it?

She crept forward cautiously, noting her surroundings. She turned, her eyes carefully scanning the parking garage. It was empty. She knew from experience that gunshots inside her isolated apartment went unheard here. She didn't think she'd be so lucky outside having fired the shot from an echoey parking garage.

Still, she moved forward, stopping at the spot where James had fallen to his knees. Mina gasped. There was a large blot of blood on the ground. She'd hit him alright, and he was hurt pretty bad. Mina kicked leaves over the bloody spot.

Then, she started running. As the sun went down under the horizon, and a dark haze began to form, Mina felt doubt. She couldn't see him anymore. He had to be out here somewhere, right?

Find him, now!

Mina could hear the sharp, angry voice of Lacose, her long-gone love.

"Oh, I'll find him," Mina swore under her breath. *If I have to look all night. I'll find James Friesen.*

33

MINA

Mina had walked for what seemed like a mile when a noise to her right stopped her short.

"Looking for someone?" a deep male voice broke into the stillness of the night.

Mina gasped and spun around. She smelled cigarette smoke and her brain registered that there was a person smoking it. She knew it was not the voice of Lacose.

Kill him now and be on your way, Lacose hissed.

"Hello?" Mina said cautiously. Her eyes fell on a heavyset man who was a few inches taller than Mina. He stood assessing her coolly, cigarette held between fingers, his hand dangling beside him, the red fire on the end of the cigarette becoming a focal point in the now dark night.

Mina froze, wondering what he knew.

It was then that she saw the slick black sheet covering what she could only assume was James' body. *Oh, God, is that James?* she wondered. The man was standing protectively in front of the sheet—she thought now that it must be a tarp.

Mina held her breath and waited.

Kill him now when he least expects it! Lacose yelled at her.

The man stared back at her.

"What are you doing out here?" Mina asked.

"Closet smoker," his voice drifted to her through the darkening night. "I come out here every night to get away from the missus and smoke. I like to have a long, uneventful time to myself. Most nights it *is* uneventful. Tonight, not so much."

"What did you see?" Mina asked.

Kill him now! Lacose shouted angrily.

When the man didn't answer, Mina tried a different question. "What's under the tarp?"

"Enough to know what happened," he replied, his gaze steely as he looked into her eyes. His foot tapped the lump under the black tarp.

"You just keep a tarp out here?" She was still trying to keep her voice casual. Her brain was trying to calculate her next move, but it felt muddled. She was grasping for her next most logical words.

The man snorted. "Gets awful muddy out here when it rains, and I have to have a place to go. If you knew the missus, you'd understand." His eyes fell to Mina's hand that she held at her side. In it, she held a gun. "You gonna kill me too?"

"Is he dead?" Mina asked. Her brain cleared and she felt disappointed. That would ruin the plan.

"You tell me. You're the one who shot him."

"So, you saw that?" Mina confirmed.

The man smirked.

"What do you want?" Mina asked. There was no need to play games. They had already wasted too much time.

"Everything you got." The man's smile meanly pulled up into a sneer.

Mina lifted the gun. She pointed it at his forehead. She watched the smirk fall from his face.

The man lifted his hands. "I didn't actually see nothin.' I

swear. You can take your boyfriend. No one will ever be the wiser, eh?"

"No deal," Mina said, feeling cold and calculated. She took a few steps forward with the gun still pointed at his head. "What's your name?"

"T-Travis," the man stuttered.

"Well, Travis. You were in the wrong place at the wrong time." Mina grabbed her cell phone from her back pocket and dialed a number without taking her eyes off Travis.

"Hello?" she put the phone up to her ear.

She paused.

"Are you in the area, Sis?" Mina asked.

She paused.

"I need you to ping my location and come find me. I'm about to kill a man." Mina hung up the phone and put it back in her pocket.

"No! You don't have to—" Travis gasped as he lunged for the gun.

Mina fired the gun and hit Travis squarely between the eyes. His eyes went from shock to glazed over in a matter of seconds. She watched as his legs buckled underneath him and he fell face-first into the soft ground. His body hit with a soft thump sound.

"Damn, I'm a good shot," Mina gloated with no remorse. But she couldn't celebrate for long. Someone was bound to have heard that gunshot. It was the second shot of the night. She looked up but could not see the apartments on the second and third floor, though she knew they were there. Someone must have heard something.

She quickly pulled back the tarp to uncover James. So much blood had already soaked through his t-shirt on his shoulder. Mina checked his pulse. He was alive. That was something, at least.

"I need to get him back inside!" Mina felt angry and impatient. "But how? He's triple the size of me!" She had an answer for that. Help was on the way, but she couldn't sit around and wait.

Mina covered James back up and rolled his body, so he was now inside the tarp, wrapped up like a burrito. She grasped the tarp at his ankles and tried to pull.

"I'm not strong enough," she said aloud, feeling surprised by that.

She pulled with all her might and slowly dragged his body an inch. This must have rubbed against James' gunshot wound, which must have hurt, because she heard him whimper.

"What's that, James? Does it hurt? Guess you'll learn your lesson for the next time you decide to run," Mina said mockingly, thinking he might just hear her. She dropped his feet and kicked him in the side. She heard air escape his lips from under the tarp. He did not fully wake up.

She picked up her phone and hit redial. Mina didn't have any family. But bonds were more powerful when you got to *choose* your family.

She listened to the phone ring. When Mina heard the voice answer, she started talking without so much as a greeting.

"How close are you?"

Mina listened to the answer, feeling relieved.

"Pulling into the parking lot now," came the reply.

"Thanks, Mazy," Mina said, looking at the name on the phone screen. Then she hung up the phone and waited.

34

JAMES

When I came to, I noticed two things. My body was moving, but not in a graceful way like floating on water. Nor was I floating on heavenly clouds. I was still alive. If the jerky start-and-stop way my body moved was any indication, I would end up back on the ground at any time.

It occurred to me that I could use this to my advantage, but the pain in my shoulder was so intense, I thought I might throw up or black out at any minute. The second thing I noticed was the voices—two of them, and only one voice was Mina's.

"Mess with his investigation—that's what you were sent in to do. To hide evidence and re-route things if they got too close," Mina grunted with effort. "Not to sleep with him, and certainly not to get him fired!"

"What's the big deal, anyway? You wanted him off the case. Now he's off the case—for good." This was a voice I did not know.

"God, Mazy, are you stupid? If he goes out as a PI, he doesn't have to get permission or run anything by a supervisor anymore. Do you realize how much quicker he can solve this thing? Jackson is *not* stupid. He was one of the best detectives on the force."

"But I'm stupid? You just killed a man because he saw you in the woods. Who's the stupid one now?"

"I had to," Mina stated calmly. "There was no other option."

"Clearly, that makes it okay to kill a man," the new voice said sarcastically.

"I'm containing our problem," Mina replied coolly.

"*You* are? Only *you*? And when did this become *our* problem? You got yourself into this. You know I supported you when you killed your dad. But that was self-defense. I don't know how I feel about murder for the sake of convenience."

"Then leave," came Mina's harsh reply.

"Okay, have fun with your little problem…"

I felt my feet and lower body hit the cold Earth. "Ow!" I moaned.

"He's awake! Shit!" Mina mumbled.

I could hear loud footsteps trampling through the leaves on the ground. There was silence for a minute. Then I heard a noise that gave me hope. Sirens wailed in the distance. I couldn't distinguish between police, ambulance, or fire sirens. All I knew was that help was finally on its way.

Now was my chance. I took a deep breath and tried to yell.

"Shut it!" Mina hissed. I felt a hand push the tarp over my face, making it difficult to breathe. Then, I felt a small fist hit my shoulder through the tarp. Pain hit so hard that I felt myself begin to black out again. I fought to regain consciousness. My last thought was wondering why I was in so much pain. I remembered that I'd been shot. Right in that shoulder she had punched.

The pain began to throb intensely around my shoulder and upper arm. I had glimpsed the dark night before I'd passed out the first time, when she shot me, and I had one thought before I passed out again now.

It's nighttime. Everyone around here is settling in for the night. Which meant that even if I could stay conscious, the likelihood of my rescue was slim.

35

MINA

"Breathe, Mina, breathe," Mina whispered to herself. It seemed like her brain was making its way through a cloud. She was only vaguely aware of what had happened since the time she lifted the gun and killed Travis. She was normally so good under pressure. In fact, she prided herself on how good she was.

The sirens were unraveling her nerves. There was no way she could carry James back to the apartment by herself. Mazy had left her. There was no getting Mazy back when she was like this. Mina had seen that anger in Mazy's eyes before.

What the hell are you doing? Lacose yelled in her ear. *Move it! You're about to get busted.*

"What should I do?" Mina asked quietly.

Do something, anything so you don't get caught! came the answer.

Mina squinted through the darkness, peering down toward the back of this property—most likely owned by the apartment company. She could see a nice sloping hill just a few feet away. Judging from the level of darkness and shadows, she'd bet she could roll James down there and no one would find him before morning. Mina could come back once the sirens left. She'd have a plan by then.

With all her strength, she rolled James, tarp and all, down the hill. She watched him roll, then heard him fall.

36

JAMES

I became aware that my body was moving. I was rolling. Then I was rolling faster. My stomach lurched as I began to fall for seconds. In those seconds of free falling, I felt my life flash before my eyes.

I saw Paige leaned over her shopping cart, talking to baby Anna. I could only see her slim figure and reddish-brown hair. But when she straightened and looked up at me, my heart burst with instant love. The connection was so powerful, I knew I'd do anything to have this woman in my life forever.

I saw my first date with Paige. She walked into the restaurant, white snowflakes resting on her hair. Her eye makeup was done in a "cat-eye" style, as she called it. That night had been light and fun. She'd gotten so ridiculously drunk by the end of the night—the only evidence that she had been nervous to be with me—and I had played the perfect gentleman and dropped her off without so much as a kiss goodnight.

But I couldn't sleep that night thinking about her. I'd gone right back over there that next morning. I couldn't stop myself. We made love for the first time.

I married her a few short months later in a snowy garden. I

knew better than to rush in. But I was head-over-heels in love with her. I loved Anna too. Anna was the daughter I never thought I'd have. I was in love with our little family.

I remembered when I'd reconnected with Paige again—in a different grocery store. Fate kept shoving us together, despite my attempts at self-sabotage. I worked with her to find our missing Anna.

I had married Paige a second time in a beautiful outdoor wedding. That was the day Anna came home to us. Paige had made me a father. I had fulfilled every goal in life I'd ever had. Paige would never doubt how much I loved her.

My memories abruptly stopped as I hit the ground hard. My whole body instantly hurt. My temple throbbed and my whole face stung. I tried to open my eyes but couldn't immediately see. I put a hand up to wipe my face and managed to open one eye. My hand was marred with blood. My head was bleeding profusely.

I closed my eyes and welcomed the merciful darkness.

37

MINA

She heard him fall. The sound James' body made as it hit the ground convinced her that he'd fallen off a ledge. Had she dumped him in a ravine?

"Oh well," she sighed. Nothing she could fix now. Her eyes fell on the gun she still held in her hand.

Wipe the prints, Lacose commanded her.

"Right," Mina answered. She carefully folded the gun into her shirt and wiped every inch of it. It would have to work.

Now, go throw it over by the guy you killed earlier, Lacose instructed.

Mina's heart thudded in her chest. Had she already forgotten about that? Killing that man was hazy. Well, she couldn't undo that now. But as she retraced her steps to the man now lying motionlessly with blood pouring out of his head, she felt remorse.

There's no time for feelings, Mina! Cover your tracks! Lacose shouted at her.

Mina placed the gun close enough to the man's right hand, it might have looked like he had offed himself. Maybe if they found James, they might assume the man had shot James, then shot himself. The bullets would match up.

Satisfied with this plan, Mina quietly took a step backward.

Grab the cigarette, Lacose said.

This made Mina hesitate. "What?" she asked aloud.

The cigarette. It's your backup plan in case you get caught.

It was brilliant. Mina scanned the area for the cigarette the man had been smoking and found it, half-smoked. She picked it up and held it between her fingers.

She turned and slowly, quietly took steps through the dark wooded area, looking at the ground for evidence that she or Mazy had been there. Fresh fall leaves littered the ground so there were no footsteps.

So intent was she on surveying the ground that she didn't see the officer standing at the entrance of the parking garage until it was too late.

38

STEPHEN

As Stephen sat on the crowded plane and pretended to sleep, he reviewed the last conversation he'd had with Paige shortly before he left. He needed to be sharp and remember everything.

Focus, Paige. Are there any other details you might have missed? Stephen had asked.

No, Paige had answered. *I've told you everything three times now.*

Paige, do you recognize anyone on this list? he'd asked her, setting the list down in front of her.

Paige had leaned forward and studied the list intently. She'd shook her head. *No. No one on this list is familiar.*

Okay, I've done background checks and plan to interview them the best I can. Don't worry, I'll get to the bottom of this. Jackson and I will find James.

I hope you do. Tears had formed and dropped down her cheeks.

Damn those tears. Stephen would do anything for her not to cry.

In the time before he'd left, Stephen had contacted Michael Sampson and Latoya Johnson and interviewed them via Zoom. They had all the right reactions. By studying their voice inflections and facial twitches, they appeared genuinely surprised to hear James was missing and claimed to not know him, having not met him in person. Stephen would interview Marilyn Cho and Peter Smith in Canada face-to-face.

When he arrived in Canada, Stephen stepped from the plane to the runway hallway. He could feel the cold air seep through and shivered a bit, though he didn't know if that was from the temperature drop or from the memories of when he was last here.

It was here where he'd met James Friesen for the first time. For all his years on the force, and his pride in being a good judge of character, Stephen had missed the tell-tale signs that James had addiction problems. He refused to admit to himself that James was clean at the time, which was why Stephen didn't see it.

Stephen had a firm belief that once an addict, always an addict. He thought about that often in the early days of leaving his daughter with Paige and James. If he were honest with himself, truly honest, he'd admit James was a good guy, but no guy would ever be good enough for the woman he'd almost proposed to or the daughter she'd given him.

Stephen walked out of the airport and into a dark, frozen tundra. Now, his shiver was due to the cold. He'd forgotten how shockingly cold Canada was, even in the fall. Canada was not his favorite place. This was the place where he'd tracked down Paige after he'd spent almost a year in a coma. Nothing good had come out of this place before. He hoped this time would be a different story.

He didn't have time to ruminate over the whole experience because he had spotted the white Toyota Tacoma Jackson told him he would be driving. It was a few years old, but it was clearly in good condition. As Stephen walked closer, the window rolled down.

"Stephen Wilton?" a deep voice asked.

Stephen stopped but his eyes narrowed with caution. "Who's asking?"

"I'm J. Jackson," the man said. His dark eyes looked serious as he pulled his ID out of his wallet and showed it to Stephen.

Stephen nodded. "Thanks, man. I appreciate that." He pulled the door open.

"And?" Jackson asked, his tone stopping Stephen.

Stephen paused. "Oh, right. Fair." He pulled out his US Marshal ID.

Jackson whistled. "Fancy. Get in."

Stephen got in the truck. "I know it's late. I can't thank you enough for picking me up." Stephen had come in on the redeye. The heater in Jackson's truck was on high, and Stephen put his hands out to thaw them, having forgotten gloves.

"I don't sleep so well," Jackson admitted. "Anything new?" he asked, keeping his eyes on the road.

"To be honest, I don't know what you know and don't know. Maybe tell me what you know, and I'll fill in the missing details?" Stephen stated directly.

"Okay. All I know is Paige called and asked me to look into James' disappearance—only it wasn't the first time. Do you know about his history?"

"Yeah, I know," Stephen responded.

"I was dismissive. I was in the middle of a case. Two bodies had washed up on shore. It was similar to the way a body had washed up on shore when Lacose was alive. Weirded me out—"

"Right, so back to James?" Stephen prompted. Lacose was the last subject Stephen wanted to talk about. He tried not to think about the shoot-out he'd had with the escaped murderer and former lieutenant of the police services.

Unbidden, a memory surfaced of Lacose in the safe house, screaming after the glass shattered and he fell over the edge and down five stories. Only when Lacose hit the ground did the screams abruptly cut off.

Stephen himself had almost joined Lacose, but Paige had grabbed his arm and managed to maneuver him back up and into the safe house. He hadn't thought about that for almost a year. Being here, in this place, it was harder to block it all out.

"Right. Sorry. I didn't believe her. I believed James was on a bender again. I told her I couldn't help until she put in a formal report. By the time she decided to do that, it was too late. I had already been let go."

"Yeah, been there, done that," Stephen laughed humorlessly.

"You got let go over a girl, too?" Jackson glanced at Stephen,

"Yeah, actually. My daughter. She had been kidnapped. My commanding officer ordered me off the case. I refused to listen, so he let me go."

"Worked out okay for you," Jackson said dryly.

"Yeah, well, I got lucky. I don't take orders as well as I should."

"So, they *promoted* you to a US Marshal," Jackson laughed. "I wasn't so lucky."

"Oh?" Stephen asked.

"I was messing around with a girl at work," Jackson grinned sheepishly.

"What?" Stephen laughed this time. "Aren't you old enough to know better?"

"Yeah... but there's something about this girl. I was drawn to her. Couldn't keep my hands off her. I don't think I really care that it got me fired, either. I think a part of my love of the job died when Lacose did. Not because of Lacose exactly—I had no love for *him*. Just that you and Paige figured him out, and I didn't have a clue. I was blind. I didn't see it. I felt like I'd lost my touch." Jackson shook his head.

"And now?" Stephen asked.

Jackson shrugged. "I'm a damn good detective. I'm just a little burned out. I kept missing stuff. Leads kept drying up. It was starting to feel like it was time to get out."

"But you're going PI?" Stephen asked. He felt a little concerned that he had teamed up with a burned-out detective to look for James. Maybe Stephen should have started with the police services.

"Yeah," Jackson grinned. "It took me two days to decide I was bored out of my mind and needed to do something. I've filled out my paperwork online to make my company legal."

"Congrats, man!" Stephen said.

"Thanks. So, where to first?" Jackson asked.

"Well, I need to interview a few witnesses who knew James was coming in and we need to get that footage from the airport. In the meantime, let's start at James' company and talk face to face with Gilly Vance. I get the feeling he's hiding something."

Jackson nodded and skillfully maneuvered the truck around. "I'll drop you at the hotel and pick you up around eight a.m. Place won't be open until then."

"Was she worth it?" Stephen asked.

"Too soon to tell," Jackson responded with a grin. "I met you before, by the way. The night you put that call in to nine-one-one. Brilliant idea, by the way. You just left the phone on while Lacose confessed to everything... I was one of the officers who responded that night."

"Well, thanks for coming to our aid," Stephen said, remembering his relief when police services showed up. "My life was flashing before my eyes. I thought Lacose had us cornered that night, for sure."

Jackson nodded. "You think we'll find James?"

Stephen shrugged, an ominous feeling in his gut. "I think we'll find him." He didn't have the heart to finish the thought they were both thinking. *Who knows if we'll find him alive?*

39

MINA

"Oh, officer! You scared me!" Mina's surprise was real enough as she stepped out of the tree cover to the parking garage.

The officer frowned at her. "What are you doing out there?"

Mina waved her cigarette at him, acting sheepish. "I just stepped around the corner to smoke. The wind blew it out. I was headed back to my apartment to grab a light." There was no way the officer would buy that. But Mina held his steady gaze.

"Did you hear the shots that were fired?" he asked suspiciously.

Mina made her eyes big. "No. I—there were shots fired?"

"You'd better go on inside, miss. We got several complaints that two shots were fired here tonight. We're about to search the area. You didn't see anything out there?" The officer peered hard at her.

Mina shook her head and fake shuddered. "Do you know what's happening?"

"Not yet, ma'am." The officer put his hand on his gun. "Please move indoors and alert authorities immediately if you see anything."

"Yes, sir," Mina said. She exhaled the breath she had been holding as she walked at a normal pace back to her apartment. Once inside, she locked the door, took her clothes off, stuck them in the washing machine, and turned on the hot water.

She threw the bedsheets where she and Lacose had spent their last night together into the washing machine. It had already filled up with soapy water and was about to start agitating.

Next, she turned on the shower, jumped in, and let the hot water wash all the blood, grime, and evidence off her hands and body. Though she was getting tired, Mina forced herself to think about what to do next. With the badges patrolling outside the apartment, it was going to be harder to get James back.

Harder, but not impossible. Since she'd already been spotted once, Mina knew she needed to be careful not to be spotted again. The police would eventually go home. Mina would wait all night if she needed. She'd get James back at any cost.

When she was done in the shower, she scrubbed the apartment from top to bottom. She hadn't cleaned it after she'd lost Lacose. She couldn't bear to. She felt she could smell his scent everywhere and his presence was still alive in this place.

But she couldn't afford a search that would reveal DNA linking her to Lacose or to James.

"Never forgotten, my love," she whispered.

40

MINA

Mina waited until she was sure the whole apartment building above her was asleep. At least, everyone in her part of the world. Here, in the apartments, there was a quiet stillness. With the exception of Mina, of course.

Mina had paced the apartment for hours trying to come up with a plan. But all logical plans ended with *wait*. She would simply wait until the early hours of the morning to go get James. Maybe by then, she would be able to get him on his feet and he would simply walk back to the apartment.

It was not a logical plan, but Mina's brain was getting tired. She picked up her cell phone and dialed the number she knew by heart. It was her ninth call. Mazy just needed some time. She had to forgive Mina. Mazy always came through for her.

Mina slumped down into a chair as she listened to the phone go to voicemail. Mazy wasn't answering. Mina looked at her watch. It was just after one in the morning. Mazy was probably just asleep. Mina was going to have to come up with a plan all by herself. Not like Mazy had been any help up to this point, anyway.

What if she actually called in an ambulance? James had been

in and out of consciousness. If he came to, Mina could claim James was delirious and that she was the doting girlfriend who had found him shot in the woods. Once they doctored him back to health, she could take him home at gunpoint.

Mina's heart sank. She didn't have a gun anymore. Did they find the gun she threw in the forest? The gun that had belonged to Lacose? What would they make of it when they tracked it back to Lacose?

Mina chewed her fingernail.

You have to let James go, Mina. He's too dangerous for you now, Lacose spoke into her ear.

"No!" she snapped. "I can fix this. I can come up with a plan. There's always a better plan."

Mina was on her feet now. Tears, masked as rage, streamed down her face.

Let him go, Mina, Lacose said again.

"I won't!" Mina shrieked. She wiped the snot that dripped from her nose. "I will see this through. You'll see. You'll be so proud of me. You'll never doubt me again after that!"

Mina collapsed into the chair and sobbed hysterically. Mina didn't fail. Mina succeeded at everything she put her hands to. Her plans always worked out. Because if they didn't, what value did she have on this Earth?

41

PAIGE

The pains started shortly after midnight.

"Oh!" Paige groaned as she woke. She tried to get comfortable. She couldn't. No matter what position she was lying in, she felt crampy and miserable. Then she sat up suddenly.

"No, no, no!" she whimpered. She remembered this pain. It was the type of pain a mother forgot after having a child because it was so acute and so dreadful, no mother would ever have another child if they carried the memory of the pain with them. At least, that's what Paige thought in this moment.

All memories about Braxton-Hick's contractions or tracking how long between pains flew out of Paige's mind as she began to panic. She threw back the covers and got out of bed. That took some effort because of the pain her body felt.

Her eyes fell on the small bag, packed with her basic necessities, that sat by her door. At least James had the presence of mind to help her pack it the week before he'd left.

Sometimes twins come early, he'd said. *I read about this. We need to be ready.*

But James wasn't here. At that thought, Paige began to cry.

"James, where are you?" she whispered as she slowly got dressed, all the while taking inventory of her body. She wondered if it was smart to drive. Especially with Anna in the car.

Anna! What in the world would she do with Anna? Anna could not be in the room while she was in labor.

Her nearest relative or friend was two hours away. She texted Brandi Burnett.

Paige: *The babies are coming, and I need help. Can you come?*

Still moving slowly, but now fully dressed, Paige moved to the door. With effort, she picked up her backpack and went to Anna's room. Gently, she shook her sleeping child.

"Anna, you need to wake up," Paige tried to keep her voice calm.

Anna gasped and cried out when she saw Paige.

"No!" she screamed. It was clear Anna wasn't seeing her mom but some dream-like version of her mom.

"Anna, honey. It's me. It's mommy. You need to get up," Paige rubbed her child's shoulder gently.

Anna scrambled back from Paige's hand until her back was against the wall. She put her hands up to her face and cried soft whimpers.

Paige felt her own tears run down her face. She knew Anna was reliving a night that never should have happened. A night that no three-year-old child should ever have to remember. The night Carley Smith had been killed. Paige had always suspected that Anna had witnessed the murder, though she'd been hiding in the armoire. The therapist assured Paige there was no way Anna would remember that at such a young age. Eventually, the nightmares would stop. Paige wasn't so sure.

"Anna, it's me, your mommy," Paige tried again. After

several minutes, Anna's glazed eyes focused on Paige and registered recognition.

"Mommy?" Anna whispered. She crawled to Paige and cuddled up to her.

"Anna, we need to go somewhere," Paige kept her voice calm and quiet. "Everything is okay, but we need to take a car ride."

"Are the babies coming?" Anna asked.

Paige was often astounded by Anna's reasoning abilities that superseded her three years.

"Yes, I think they are, Anna."

Anna's blond, curly hair was sticking up in some places and frizzing in others. Her pink and blue striped pajamas smelled like baby sweat. "Can you help mommy out and put a pair of clothes in your backpack?"

"Can I bring my blankie?" Anna asked hopefully as she grabbed her favorite soft yellow blanket she always slept with.

"Yes, bring that and pick one stuffed animal," Paige commanded softly, eyeing Anna's bed that was full of stuffed animals.

Anna did as she was instructed. "Okay, let's go." Anna got up and put her hand in Paige's hand, looking brave, having forgotten her earlier panic.

"Run and go potty before we leave," Paige instructed her as she picked up the backpack.

Paige got them into the car and paused before driving off. She wasn't that close to her co-workers at the vet clinic but there was one person she thought she would trust to watch Anna until Brandi arrived.

Paige dialed Marge's number and listened to several rings, well aware it was sometime after midnight. Marge finally answered.

"Marge, I'm so sorry to disturb you. It's just that I think I'm in labor and my husband is out of town. I need someone to keep an eye on Anna…" Paige listened as Marge agreed to meet her at the hospital.

Paige tried to focus on the road through the tears that blurred her vision and pain that gripped her mid-section.

"James, where are you?"

42

MINA

"James, where are you?" Mina whispered in the darkness. The leaves crunched softly under her black ballerina shoes. No amount of walking softly could alleviate the noise. An occasional wind whipped from the north and chilled Mina.

The only thing she had going for her was the cover of a moonless night. She had dressed in head-to-toe black. She knew she blended perfectly into the darkness.

She was now standing in the exact spot where James must have fallen earlier that evening. Mina took two steps back and looked upward. In retrospect, it was a terrible place to push someone down the hill. While the hill sloped near the top, there was an abrupt drop off. Which meant James would have fallen at least three feet.

Only James was not here.

Maybe she was wrong about the location. It had been dark when she rolled him. Every landmark was starting to look like the last. But then she saw it. The tarp. It must have unraveled. James would have kept rolling. Falling about right in this spot.

Mina bent down, peering hard at the ground. The dark night gave nothing away. The ground seemed wet with dew. She brushed her hand against the cold, damp Earth. She was surprised that the dew seemed to darken her fingertips.

"Looking for something, miss?"

Mina screamed and lost her balance, falling on her bottom.

"James?" Mina tried to peer upward, but a strong light was pointed right in her face.

"I'm Officer Keeney. What are you looking for, eh?" a deep, burly voice asked again.

Mina got on her feet and put her hand over her face to block the light.

"I'm looking for my friend, James. He went out for a run and never came back. Have you seen anyone out here?" Mina tried to keep her voice casual. Her heart thumped erratically in her chest. She was cursing herself for using James' name.

"A run?" the officer's voice sounded suspicious.

Mina shrugged. "We got in a fight. He went to let off some steam."

"You know what I think?" the officer asked rhetorically. "I think you're returning to the scene of a crime."

"There's been a crime?" Mina attempted to sound fearful.

"Yeah, I'm gonna need you to put your hands behind your back," the officer said.

"For what?" Mina asked desperately. She attempted to laugh. "Taking a walk outside?"

"Turn around and place your hands behind your back," the officer repeated, sounding angry.

"Can you just show me a badge, please?" Mina requested, trying to take the upper hand. "I'm sure this is just a big misunderstanding."

The officer kept the flashlight up and reached for his badge on his belt. He flashed it.

"Thank you," Mina said. She could hear how calm her voice sounded. "Now, can you please tell me why you feel the need to arrest me?"

"Trespassing on private property. Suspicious behavior. Returning to the scene of a crime," the officer cited. This time, he would hear no protests. He roughly grabbed Mina's arm and turned her around.

"Hey!" she yelped. But Mina was more surprised than hurt. She allowed herself to be cuffed now. "You keep saying returning to the scene of a crime. Have you found my friend? Is he okay?"

"I think you know very well what's happening. To think I actually believed you when I saw you earlier. I really thought you were smoking. But I don't think you were in those woods to smoke."

"I think I'm going to need to talk to a lawyer," Mina said as she allowed herself to be led down a path and up a gently sloping hill. They walked directly toward a police services car.

"Watch your head," the man said as he stuffed Mina into the back seat.

Mina had never been in the back of a police car before. At least, not as a criminal. She waited until the man had shut his door and was behind the wheel of the car.

"You know it's a myth, right?" Mina asked.

"What is?" the officer asked wearily.

"Criminals only return to the scene of the crime eighteen-point-two percent of the time. Most people really aren't dumb enough to try that."

And yet, you did, Mina, came the harsh, critical voice of Lacose. She wished she could shut him up sometimes.

The officer snorted.

Mina stopped talking and watched as the lights of Winnipeg flashed by in a blur. She knew the way to the Police Service of Winnipeg. She had just never been transported there in this manner.

43

JAMES

I felt my body moving but not of my own accord. My hands and feet hung limply. I didn't even have the energy to open my eyelids.

Someone was carrying me. I tried to groan—to let the person know I was capable of walking by myself. But was I capable? I felt drugged. Alarmed at the thought, I tried to move, twitch, or jerk—to do something. I could not.

We finally stopped moving and I heard a car door open. My body flopped into the back seat.

"Damn, he's heavy!" stated a man's voice I didn't recognize.

"I told you I would help!" This was a female voice. It was not the voice of Mina Martin.

"Get in," came the reply.

"But I—" the female voice faltered. "I did my part. I'm out. You promised."

"Oh no, I'm not letting you out of my sight. Get in!"

With no other argument, the talking ceased, and I heard two car doors shut and the crunch of gravel under the tires of the car as they backed out of wherever this was.

I worked hard to open my eyes. I felt them flicker, but they burned when they took in the soft light from the car dashboard. Before my eyes shut again, I made a few observations. It was night. I was, indeed, in the back seat of a vehicle. There were two people in the front seats. Both were dressed in black. They were both wearing black stocking caps.

My mind seemed to be waking up, and it spun with thoughts that led to anxiety and torture. I still could not move my hands or feet. Were they bound? I couldn't tell, so I tried my fingers first. Nothing happened. It felt like my body was paralyzed. This was worse than being kidnapped by Mina Martin. At least I knew where I stood with Mina. There was no question of whether I would die in the end. I knew Mina's plan.

What if this would end worse than death? Why had torture become my biggest fear?

44

MINA

Mina was sitting in an interrogation room. The same room where she'd often observed suspects from the other side of the glass. In those days, she was often called in to watch for behavior patterns or "tells." She had watched for irregularities in stories or inconsistencies in the details criminals gave.

Mina knew better than to say a word right now. If she did speak, she needed to be careful. On her game. Strategic, even. She had to outsmart whoever was watching her behind that glass. Only, it was after three in the morning. Mina knew they had a skeleton crew.

That's why she was surprised to see two men walk into the room. One man looked tired, like he'd woken up and drove in for this conversation. He was tall and thin with a white mustache. His face wore a kind expression, but his brown eyes were dark and firm.

"I'm Chief Coppernet," he introduced himself. The officer who'd arrested Mina followed him in and shut the door behind them. "You met Officer Keeney."

"You must be new," Mina said kindly, trying a tactic other

than silence. "Neither of you worked at police services when I was here."

The officer's eyes flicked nervously to his chief. The chief regarded Mina with uncertainty. They both looked caught off guard.

"I used to work for police services. I'm Mina. Mina Martin. I—"

"Shit! You're Mina Martin? You're like a legend around here. You created the crime analysis system we use," Chief Coppernet said, letting his guard down.

Mina laughed in actual delight. "I did. I wouldn't call myself a legend though…"

"No, really. You're like a big deal. I've been briefed on the before and after. Your system closed the gap on open cases and reduced the turnaround time for closing cases," Chief Coppernet insisted. He relaxed into his seat more. He shot his officer an annoyed look.

Which is why I had to send in Mazy to be my eyes and ears, Mina thought. Her jaw clenched at the thought of Mazy. She never thought Mazy would turn on her.

The officer looked uncomfortable and looked expectantly at his chief. "Sir, I found her wandering the forest where the one-forty…"

"She knows what that means," the chief said gruffly. "Speak plainly."

"Right, it was the second time I'd seen her in the same location tonight. I thought she'd returned to the scene of a crime," the officer seemed to lose steam as he spoke, and his cheeks took on a pink hue.

"Is it a crime to walk around at night, officer?" the chief asked sharply.

"Well, no, but—"

Mina giggled a little. "That's what I wondered, too."

The chief shared a smirk with her. "Maybe you can clear this up once and for all. Ms. Martin, why were you in the woods? Start with the first sighting," the chief made air quotes with his fingers as he said the word *sighting*.

Mina cleared her throat. "I was smoking," she pretended to be embarrassed as she made the admission. "Filthy habit, I know."

The chief nodded. "And the second time?"

"I was looking for my friend. He went out for a run. It was late." Mina shrugged, feigning embarrassment. "I got worried when he didn't come back. He's a trail runner. He didn't answer my text, so I went out to make sure he didn't twist an ankle."

"Should we file a missing persons report?" the officer asked, now trying to act helpful.

Mina knew he was new. Mina shook her head. "As you were putting me in the car, my phone buzzed. He actually made it back just fine. Miscommunication. I thought he was coming back to my place. He ran home—not back to my place. All a silly mistake."

"Hmm," Officer Keeney folded his arms and sat back.

"I see no reason to hold you any longer, Ms. Martin. Sorry for the inconvenience." The chief shot the officer a cloudy look. "Officer Keeney here will escort you back home. Try to get some sleep in what's left of the night."

"Will do, sir." Mina got up and allowed the officer to uncuff her hands from behind her back.

Before Mina could fully exit the room, the chief stopped her again. "You know, your old position just opened back up. We could really use you back on the force, Mina. Would you consider it?"

Mina inhaled sharply. Her reaction was all too real. She couldn't change the direction her life had gone after Lieutenant Lacose had kidnapped her, forced her to become part of his team, then fell in love with her. She'd chosen him and it had changed the side she was on forever.

"Too many memories," Mina shuddered. She didn't have to fake her reactions now.

"I was afraid you might say that," Chief Coppernet said sadly. "Well, please let us know if you ever change your mind."

"I will, sir. Thank you." Mina shook his hand for good measure and walked out the door with Officer Keeney.

"I'm so sorry, Ms. Martin," the officer immediately apologized when she was in the car.

"Apology accepted." Mina's heart hammered in her chest. This had been close. Too close.

Once back at the apartment, Mina cooperated as the officer helped her out of the car. She casually walked to her apartment. Walking an officer to her somewhat hidden apartment was the absolute last thing she wanted to do. But she could see no other solution here. She had to play this out.

She opened her door and stood uncertainly. She had cleaned her place and felt confident nothing was amiss.

"Would you like a drink?" Mina asked as she held the door open wider. She watched the officer's eyes flick around the room.

He shook his head and took a step back. Mina had banked on the fact that an officer would say *no* to a drink while on duty.

"Sorry for all the trouble and confusion tonight, Mina," the officer said.

"Not at all." Mina smiled and faked a yawn.

"I'm glad you found James—isn't that who you said you were looking for?"

"Thank you. Me too." Mina quickly shut and locked the door and silently threw her whole body into a convulsive fit. It was only a matter of time before the officer put together that there was a missing report for a man named James.

"But wait," Mina whispered, trying to calm down. "No one is looking for James yet."

ADDISON MICHAEL

Oh yes, they are, Lacose snapped at her. *You called Paige earlier today, remember? You better believe she called it in by now.*

"Right," Mina cursed softly and felt sweat trickle down her back. She started packing a bag with enough belongings for her to stay on the run for a while. Then she rushed to leave.

Stop! Lacose commanded sharply.

Mina had reached for the door to leave her apartment but then jerked her hand away like she'd been burned.

Clearly, the officer is watching you tonight. You can't risk leaving now. It would only raise suspicion. Lacose's voice was patronizing.

Mina nodded and dropped her bag. She walked to her bedroom and fell onto her bed, overwhelmed with exhaustion. The freshly washed sheets and fluffy bedspread enveloped her body. She kicked off her shoes and fell into a fevered, fitful sleep.

She slept for less than three hours before her alarm went off. She snoozed her alarm three times before she dutifully got up and got dressed for work.

She would go to work. She would act normal. But she would not be coming back to the apartment ever again.

45

PAIGE

"Mrs. Friesen, I'm Dr. Stone." A petite woman with light blond hair and green eyes stood at Paige's bedside. It was a small room with one bed, which Paige now occupied. The doctor turned and washed her hands at the sterile sink. She dried her hands and opened the cabinet above the sink. Paige watched as she opened a box of gloves and put them on.

Paige adjusted the thin sheet over her. She was wearing a hospital gown, and the room was cold.

Why aren't hospital rooms more welcoming? she wondered. There was one picture of a meadow with a field of pink flowers and a white dry erase board hanging on the wall, but that was it.

The doctor turned back to Paige.

"Hello," Paige said. For the past hour, she had been attempting to rest, but her body was too crampy and sore. She was so sure she was in labor. Once she was in the semi-lit room, the contractions seemed to stop, and Paige was able to close her eyes and rest a bit.

"Let me check you out here." Dr. Stone opened the door of the room and waived in a nurse. The nurse came in with a friendly look on her face. Paige had met this nurse earlier when she was first admitted. The nurse's name was Sarah, or Sally, but Paige couldn't quite remember which one. "Are you ready?"

"Yes," Paige answered. She allowed the poking and prodding. Then she waited quietly as the nurse took off her gloves and threw them away.

"You are dilated to about a two, but it's too early for you to be in labor. While it's true twins tend to come early, we would like you to go another week to ten days. Your blood pressure is elevated which can be a sign of preeclampsia. However, you don't have any of the other signs of that. I don't notice excess water weight or swelling. Other than the contractions—most likely Braxton Hicks—you are fine. Are you under any abnormal stress?"

"Yes," Paige said, nodding as her eyes filled with tears.

"Okay," Dr. Stone said. "How do you feel right now? Are you still having contractions?" She looked at the monitor screen to answer her question.

"I feel okay now and no, the contractions seem to have stopped," Paige admitted.

"That's good," Dr. Stone said with relief. "I'm going to send you home but with strict orders. You're on bedrest for the next few weeks with the exception of your weekly checkups. Do you have someone who can drive you?"

Paige nodded. Brandi Burnett had texted back that she was on her way. That was over an hour ago. "I have a friend on her way. She's coming in from out of town, so it might be another hour."

"That's fine," the doctor smiled kindly. "The bed is yours to rest until your friend arrives. I need you to promise me to stay in bed until your next visit. You can follow up with your OB."

Paige nodded but fought the urge to cry again. How was she going to take care of Anna and be on bedrest for the next two weeks by herself?

The doctor seemed satisfied. "Get some rest and good luck. I hope I don't see you until closer to term."

"Thanks," Paige said, but as she watched the doctor walk out of the room, she turned her head to the side and felt her tears soak the pillow.

If only James would walk through that door right now, Paige knew he would help her through this. But Paige felt afraid she would never see James again.

Paige could hear James' voice echo in her mind.

Look, bad things do happen. But they don't just happen to you or me. They happen to everyone. But the strong ones overcome. That's us. We're overcomers. We don't let the darkness of the past overwhelm us or determine our future. We let the past stay in the past and move forward.

The answer, according to James, was to give her fear to God. Right now, Paige was doing everything she could just to hang on to her sanity.

46

JAMES

My eyes flickered again. Only this time, I could see a bright light and could feel the heat from that light warming my face. I closed my eyes because the light above was so bright, it was all I could see. My head was throbbing. The light in my face hadn't helped.

I wiggled my fingers. I attempted to wiggle my toes. I tried to kick my legs. Nothing happened. I felt myself panicking.

What if I was paralyzed?

My shoulder hurt with a constant pain, but that wasn't new. Either my body was going into shock, or I was getting used to the pain. What I wasn't used to was how weak I felt. And maybe it was the light, but my body felt like it was hot enough to be on fire.

My mind moved backwards through the night to the last memories I had. The ones before I was carried here. Wherever *here* was. I tried again to open my eyes and look around. I couldn't keep my eyes opened. I remembered rolling down a hill, falling, and hitting the ground hard. I had hit my head. I remembered blacking out.

The terror over possible paralysis made me cry. I could feel the tears leak out of the corner of my eyes.

"He's awake! Shit!" A man's voice yelled loudly.

"Wha—Oh! He's crying!" That was the female voice. She sounded angry. Her voice had an accusatory tone. "I didn't sign up for this! You promised not to hurt him!"

I pried my eyes open just in time to see a needle coming my direction. I saw a large, rough-looking hand gripping a needle. This hand must belong to the man I had heard speaking.

"No… drugs…!" I forced the words out but felt the end of the word *drugs* taper off and wasn't sure if I actually spoke the whole word.

They must not have heard me because I fell unconscious again.

47

STEPHEN

"Well, I'll be damned! Mina?" Jackson's voice held surprise. He and Stephen had no more than taken a step off the elevator when he spotted the receptionist desk. It was a tall, white, regal desk that was built into a smooth curve with the words "JS Friesen Construction" in letters that looked like they were dipped in gold.

Behind the desk sat a petite, thin woman who looked to be in her early to mid-thirties. She had black hair that had been layered in a choppy haircut that made her hair flip in a trendy way around her face. Her makeup was a bit dark. Heavy black eyeliner around her eyes was drawn to a point. Were her eyes green, or was that just the dark green sparkling eyeshadow on her eyelids?

"Jackson?" Mina returned a little too brightly. Her eyes looked tired, dull, and flat. Her gaze flicked over to Stephen and back to Jackson. "What are you doing here?"

She came from around the desk and gave Jackson an awkward side hug that ended with a masculine pat on the back. Hugging clearly did not appear to come naturally to her. Though she looked happy enough to see Jackson, Stephen didn't buy it.

Stephen didn't have to be a US Marshal to see the immediate reaction on Mina's face when they had stepped off the elevator. She'd looked angry. Her eyes almost looked like her pupils had enlarged and her eye color was an instant shade of black. She was hiding it well, but she was not happy to see them. Her eyes had told him a different story. Even if only for a moment before she masked it.

"We're investigating a disappearance," Jackson stated.

"A disappearance? There's always something going on at police services..." Mina said with a smirk as her voice trailed.

"Actually, I'm not at police services anymore," Jackson said.

Stephen's eyes looked intently at Mina for her reaction.

"What happened?" Mina asked. Her eyes were wide, but something about her reaction told Stephen she already knew the answer to that.

"That's a long story." Jackson dismissed her question with a flick of his hand. "As I said, we're looking into a disappearance."

"Right," Mina agreed. She waited but when they didn't say more, she looked surprised again. "Oh, you mean the disappearance has something to do with us here? In this place?" She waved toward the business name on the desk.

"Yes." Jackson cleared his throat. "Well, we aren't sure at what point he disappeared. When was the last time you saw James Friesen?"

Stephen pulled out up a photo on his phone and watched Mina's eyes flick to it and quickly back to Jackson.

"Oh, James." Mina forced a laugh. "He never showed up to the meeting. It's typical James though. He's notorious for no-showing meetings, so I'm told."

"Wait, you knew he was coming for the acquisitions meeting?" Stephen said now.

"Well... yeah." Mina scratched the back of her head, ruffling the back of her hair in the process.

Was her neck getting red? Stephen wondered. Now she seemed a little nervous. Stephen pulled up the note on his phone and scanned the list. Mina's name was not on it. Did Gilly purposely leave her name off, or had he forgotten to mention her? Stephen added her name on his phone list and made a mental note to do a background check on her later.

"You aren't on the list of names of people who knew about the meeting that Gilly gave me," Stephen said.

Mina rolled her eyes. "Typical. You do all the work to coordinate schedules, make copies, and order food and there's not so much as an acknowledgement of hard work." Mina sounded put out and it sounded sincere.

"Did you also order him a ride from the airport?" Stephen asked.

"Oops, sounds like I missed something." Mina shrugged apologetically.

"You didn't coordinate a ride from the airport to the office?" Stephen asked again.

Mina frowned now and shook her head. "No, why?"

"He told his wife when he was on the phone with her that his ride had arrived at the airport, and he needed to let her go."

"Huh," Mina said. "I guess I figured he used to live in Canada, he could surely find his way to a meeting at the office."

"Right, and he would have, but he didn't," Jackson said again.

Mina nodded slowly, looking evenly at Jackson.

Stephen watched, feeling like this interaction was getting weirder by the moment.

"I'm sorry, guys. Was there something I could do for you? Do you need me to answer some questions or something? Can I get you on Gilly's calendar? He's off this morning." Mina went back around her desk to consult her calendar. "I'm actually not sure what time he'll be back."

"Yes, there is something you can do," Stephen stated. "I

would like contact information to Marilyn Cho and Peter Smith. Where they work, phone numbers, email addresses—whatever you have."

Mina was now looking at her computer. She grabbed post-it notes and a pen. She paused and looked at Stephen. "I don't know if I should say this—"

"Every little thing helps," Jackson cut in.

"Well, of the four people who were meeting, Marilyn and Peter had the most to gain from this sale going through quickly." Mina tapped her pen against the desk.

"Why is that?" Jackson asked.

"They are both located here in Canada. The company they work for would merge and change the name of this company to theirs. And no, I'm not at liberty to tell you the name of that company."

"Let me guess," Stephen said dryly, remembering Gilly's previous words. "It's top secret."

"Yeah," Mina smirked at him. "But what you don't know is the physical building where their offices are housed here in Canada is closing due to extenuating circumstances. They needed this building to become their home base headquarters here in Canada."

"It doesn't exactly provide a motive to take James. If anything, it seems if they picked him up from the airport, they would immediately deliver him to the meeting and place a pen in his hand."

Mina shrugged. "A company like that might have enemies who stand to lose a lot with companies merging. It's not unusual in the business world for people to have connections—some of them go pretty dark."

"Maybe," said Stephen. He still wasn't buying it. Was she working a little too hard to provide a suspect?

Mina finished writing the information and handed them two

post-it notes. "Anything else, gentlemen? I need to get to work on the company newsletter."

"Yeah, have Gilly call us when he's back in," Jackson said quickly. "You still have my number, right? I'd like to meet with him."

"Sure, Jackson. It was nice to see you again. And you— Stephen, was it? Nice to meet you." Mina peered deeply into Stephen's eyes until it was almost uncomfortable.

Stephen watched Mina until she covered her mouth and yawned. Then he followed Jackson back into the elevator. When the door closed, Stephen asked the question he'd thought was the obvious one.

"Does she always act like that?" Stephen asked abruptly.

"Who?" Jackson asked.

"Mina," Stephen replied.

"Like what?" Jackson asked.

"I don't know. Spacey at times. Angry at others. Her behavior just seemed off. Inconsistent," Stephen said with a shrug.

"No. Actually, she's usually the most put together person I know," Jackson said with a frown.

Stephen recalled the way her eyes went almost black on more than one occasion, and he shuddered.

"Weird," the men said in unison.

Before the elevator door closed, Stephen had taken out his phone, dialed a number, and was on a call with Marilyn Cho. Next, he called Peter Smith. He almost hit his head at the obvious answers they gave him. They, along with Gilly Vance, Michael Sampson, and Latoya Johnson, were all sitting up in a conference room waiting for James' arrival at the moment James went missing. And yes, even though the meeting was set for after normal business hours, they could all vouch for each other, which provided each of them with a solid alibi. Stephen would even bet he could find some video proof of them entering and leaving the building if he needed it.

"Another dead end," Stephen said as he got off the phone and climbed into Jackson's truck.

48

STEPHEN

"So, what do you make of Mina's behavior?" Stephen asked Jackson as they drove to the police services offices. Stephen needed to check in and see if they had any leads on James yet.

"No clue." Jackson shrugged. "Everyone has an off day. Speaking of an off day, maybe you should go talk to the chief alone. We aren't exactly on good terms."

"And miss a terrible, awkward situation?" Stephen grinned. "No way. You can introduce me."

"Might not lend to your credibility," Jackson muttered as he slowed his truck and pulled into the police services office.

"I've got this." Stephen flashed his US Marshal badge. "Besides, you have a legit business. They might need to call you for help someday."

Jackson grumbled as he got out of the car.

After a short flight of stairs, they found themselves in front of the new chief's office. The office was teeming with activity. It was similar to other police offices where Stephen had worked. It was one open room with desks lining the wall. In the middle of the room were various police officers, a receptionist, and a couple empty desks. A few civilians sat in chairs beside the desks of the officers.

"Can I help you?" The name on the door said *Chief Coppernet.* He stood with a scowl as he viewed Jackson.

"I'm US Marshal Stephen Wilton, and I've enlisted the help of my old friend, Jackson, to help with a case I'm looking into. I believe my office emailed you that I was coming?" Stephen flashed his badge.

Chief Coppernet kept the frown and bypassed Stephen's statement. "*Old friend*? Are you visiting, or helping solve a case, Marshal Wilton? I'm failing to make the connection of why you're here—in my precinct."

"I think that's a closed-door conversation," Stephen replied. At the chief's nod, Stephen came into the room and saw a tall, thin officer sitting in a chair. Stephen had missed him before. Jackson shut the door behind them.

The office was bigger than the conference room in his office back home, and there was plenty of space for the four of them to sit comfortably. The view next door held a brick building and the hint of a skyline just over the rooftop. The chairs in the room were all matching and clearly upscale, made of luxe leather, with rollers on the bottom.

"This is Officer Keeney," Chief Coppernet referred to the officer. "He was just about to brief me on something. I trust he's okay to stay."

Stephen shrugged and nodded. "The connection here is that I was instrumental in the takedown of Ludwig Lacose. Got the confession out of him before he locked me and your former CIO, Paige Mynart, in a shed which he had lit on fire. Jackson here showed up at the scene and took Lacose out. Saved our lives—"

"Lacose!" Officer Keeney interrupted in surprise. "Weird you bring up his name right now."

Chief Coppernet held up a hand to stop his officer from

saying more. He sat behind his desk and indicated to the remaining chairs in the room. Jackson and Stephen sat. Chief Coppernet crossed his hands over his chest.

"Why are you here now? How can I help you, Marshal Wilton?"

"Just Stephen." Stephen sat forward, perched on the edge of his seat. His knee bounced with unused energy and the feeling that something big was about to happen. "As you likely read in the email, I'm here to follow up on a missing person, James Friesen—"

"James?" Officer Keeney interrupted, looking surprised.

"Let the man finish, please," Chief Coppernet commanded.

"James Friesen landed here earlier this week to attend a business meeting at his company, JS Friesen Construction. We can't find anyone who saw him after he got off the plane, though he told his wife when he landed that his ride was there to pick him up. The company secretary, Mina Martin—"

"Mina Martin?" Officer Keeney practically shot out of his chair.

"Damnit, Keeney, take a seat and let the man finish. I know you're new to the force, but listening is an essential skill of this job," Chief Coppernet barked.

"But I really—"

"Let Stephen finish!" Chief Coppernet snapped.

Keeney's face turned red with annoyance, but he closed his mouth and sat back.

Stephen hesitated. It felt like Coppernet was trying to keep Keeney from telling them something important. "Mina Martin said she didn't send a car. So, we think whoever picked James up intercepted him at the airport and abducted him from there. We would like to request airport footage from that day to ascertain who grabbed him."

"Is that everything?" Chief Coppernet asked.

"Not quite," Stephen said. "He called his wife a few days ago to tell her he had been kidnapped, he was in Winnipeg, and he needed her to come. Only, he knew she can't get on a plane right now. She's eight-and-a-half months pregnant. Someone was coaching him on what to say—"

"Someone who wanted to get Paige here," Jackson interrupted excitedly. "What if it's not about James at all? Maybe it's about Paige."

"Does Paige have any enemies here?" Chief Coppernet asked.

"No, I showed her the list of people who knew James was coming. She didn't know any of them."

"Unless someone in that crew was loyal to Lacose—"

"For the love of God, it's Mina!" Officer Keeney exploded as he jumped to his feet. The room went silent. He finally had everyone's attention.

"Mina? What in the world does she have to do with this?" Jackson said skeptically.

"Let me tell you about last night. Shots were fired at her apartment building. We showed up at the scene and found a man dead in the woods at the back of the apartments. The gun was lying beside him. Looked like a suicide. We just got the registration back and the gun is registered to one Ludwig Lacose—"

"What?" Chief Coppernet sounded shocked.

"Yeah, that's what I came in here to tell you. It gets weirder. We staked out all night at the location where the body was found. At three in the morning, I run into Mina Martin, all dressed in black and looking for her friend, *James*. Said he went for a run and never came back so she was worried and went looking for him. Only, that was the second time I saw Mina in those woods that night. First time, she's holding an unlit cigarette and said she'd been smoking when the wind blew out her flame—"

"Mina doesn't smoke," Jackson interjected flatly. "She thought it was a filthy habit and helped me stop."

"She coulda started," Chief Coppernet suggested weakly.

"Not from the way she was holding that cigarette. Looked like she'd never touched one in her life," Officer Keeney continued. "So, I bring her in to the station last night because I think it's suspicious that she was out there *twice*, like she's returning to the scene of the crime. Chief here lets her go on account of her service to the department—"

Now Chief Coppernet looked sheepish. "I believed her. She created our crime analysis program—"

"It's a great program," Jackson interrupted with agreement.

Chief Coppernet nodded.

"Anyway," Officer Keeney continued. "I take her back to her apartment—which is really tucked away—like in a corner, by the way, didn't even know an apartment was there—when I see it." Officer Keeney took a breath.

"Well, don't stop now!" Jackson prompted.

Stephen, too, was hanging on his every word.

"She offers me a drink. I say *no*. But just before the door closes, I see something shiny peeking out from under the couch. Granted, it was a few feet away, but I swear I saw the word 'Lacose' on it. It was a police badge. That's the other thing I came to tell you, Chief. I think we need to get a warrant."

"Well, get it fast," Chief Coppernet nodded at Officer Keeney. "I want you to go search the place with these guys. Let's get to the bottom of this. The one thing we don't have is a motive. Why on earth would Mina Martin kidnap James and why would she have Ludwig Lacose's badge?"

Stephen had no idea, but he couldn't wait to call Paige to see if she had any theories.

49

PAIGE

Paige was snuggled up with Anna, who was watching a cartoon on her iPad, while Paige attempted to read. She'd read the same paragraph multiple times and couldn't comprehend what she was reading. She knew Anna was just excited that Paige was letting her snuggle on the bed with her and that it was in the middle of the day, but she knew the novelty would soon wear off.

Her friend and former psychologist, Brandi Burnett, had cancelled her patients and drove down to stay with Paige until the babies came. Right now, Brandi was grocery shopping.

Paige's phone rang. She picked up on the first ring. "Stephen? Where have you been? I've been calling you!"

"Daddy!" Anna shrieked excitedly.

Paige put it on speaker.

"Hi, daddy!" Anna called.

"Hey, Anna! How's my girl?" he asked.

"Good, watching cartoons in bed with mommy."

"What?" Stephen asked. "It's like the middle of the afternoon there."

"Mommy can't get out of bed ever again."

"I'm on bed rest," Paige said impatiently. "I need to talk to your daddy alone, Anna."

"Ohhhh!" Anna protested.

Paige took the phone off speaker and put it up to her ear. "What's happening there?"

"You'll never believe this," Stephen recapped the crazy story he'd just heard from Officer Keeney. "Do you have any idea why Mina Martin would be mixed up in all this?"

Paige was momentarily speechless. "No, Mina is my friend…" Paige was silent as she thought back to the time Lacose had broken out of prison and sent a violent message that said he was coming after Paige. They had put Paige in WITSEC after that.

Paige shuddered. She hated remembering that time. She glanced at Anna. That was the beginning of over a year of not seeing Anna. It was a period of her life she would not want to relive. Let alone think about. Still. Something rolled around in her head.

"You know," Paige said slowly. "I always wondered how Lacose had found us. He never struck me as brilliant. Just connected. He definitely misused his power. There was a lot of talk that they had somehow hacked my ankle monitor once I left the perimeter. I never believed he knew how to do that.

"But the only person I know who could've figured out a way —it never dawned on me before—is Mina Martin. She's the only person I can think of. I just can't figure out why she would've gotten mixed up with Lacose—"

"You don't know that she wasn't held against her will," Stephen broke in. "Or blackmailed."

"True," Paige mused. "It just wouldn't explain why she would be pushing his agenda forward now."

"Any chance she fell for him?' Stephen asked.

"Lacose and Mina?" Paige almost laughed aloud. "No way!"

"Stranger things have happened," Stephen defended. "She could be out for—"

"Revenge!" they said simultaneously. The realization settled uncomfortably between them.

"You know," Paige said slowly, puzzling back through her brief phone call with James, "I've replayed my conversation with James over and over again in my head. He kept saying *I mean eh... I—*"

"I mean... I, what?" Stephen interrupted excitedly. "Try to remember, exactly. I know we've talked about this already, but slow down and try to repeat the conversation word for word."

Paige closed her eyes, trying to concentrate. "He said that phrase repeatedly. At the time, I thought it was weird because it's not something he says a lot. But he said it like three times. I asked him where he was and he said, *I mean, eh... I can tell you I'm in Winnipeg.* I asked him, *Where in Winnipeg?* He said, *You just need to come. I mean, eh... I can tell you where I am when you get here.* I asked him if he wanted me to get on a plane right now, knowing he would not, and he said, *I've been kidnapped. I'm in Winnipeg. I mean, eh... I need you to come here.*"

"I mean, eh... I," Stephen said the words aloud slowly. Then he said them faster. "I mean, eh... I."

"Mina. It's a stretch, but it sounds like the word *Mina*. Dear God, Mina kidnapped James?" Paige felt horrified over the realization that James had been kidnapped to get back at Paige. It was her fault James had gone missing.

"We'll find him, Paige," Stephen seemed to read her mind. "There's no reason to suspect he's anything but alive."

Paige sniffed and the tears began to fall again.

"Hey, stop that. You need to keep your stress level down. Take it to your higher power. Isn't that what you believe now?" Stephen quoted her religious words back to her, hating to hear her cry.

"Yes," Paige agreed.

"Paige?"

"Huh?" She wiped her nose.

"We'll find him."

50

JACKSON

Jackson was dozing off when he heard a loud pounding on his door. It had taken him the better part of the night to finally relax enough to fall asleep. The day had been frustrating, to say the least. Once they'd put the pieces together, it hadn't taken long to get a warrant to search the apartment where Mina had been staying.

Officer Keeney had taken him and Stephen back there. Sure enough, they'd found Ludwig Lacose's badge exactly where Keeney had seen it. How he'd spotted it from his place at the door, and how Mina had missed it, Jackson would never know.

Other than that badge, a thorough search of Mina's *tucked-away apartment* revealed nothing. They'd dusted for prints and turned the place upside down. But her apartment was spotless. There was a spare bedroom with a contraption in the wall that looked like a window. When one side lifted, the other side locked. It didn't take a genius to ascertain what Mina might have been using that for. The lock on the outside of the door was proof of his theory.

Mina had been holding a prisoner. Not that they could find a shred of evidence that anyone had been in that room. The bed was stripped, and they'd found the linens in the dryer. The room, like the rest of the apartment, had been wiped clean.

It had been an hour before Mina's office shut down for the evening. They'd decided to split up. Officer Keeney went to JS Friesen Construction with the intention of arresting Mina. Gilly Vance told him angrily that Mina had left for lunch and had not returned to work. Officer Keeney returned to the apartment and informed them.

So, they'd had no choice but to wait there in hopes that Mina would eventually come home. Only, Mina had never showed up. It was around six that evening when they all realized their mistake. Mina had known they were onto her. She wasn't coming back to the scene of the crime. Nor did they have any idea where she would go.

Show us where you found Mina, Stephen had said to Officer Keeney. He wasn't one to give up so easily.

But Jackson felt downright defeated. This was the second person in the police services where he'd worked who had turned on him. The second guilty person he'd missed. What if he'd known subconsciously but let his feelings and emotions get in the way? He really was slipping.

Still, he followed Officer Keeney and Stephen to the spot where Keeney had picked up Mina the night before. To think, the officer had her in the police station and had let her go. Now, they might never find her again.

Well, would you look at that! Stephen had exclaimed, breaking into Jackson's personal pity party.

Jackson's eyes zeroed in on what Stephen was pointing at. It was blood. A big blot of blood. *Let's get a DNA sample.*

But Jackson didn't need to say it. Stephen was already moving. They knew whose blood they would find. Surely, if they continued on the path, they would find the owner.

They did not. They searched until sundown, walking up and down the bank of a small, dried-up riverbed, their eyes searching meticulously up and down. Then they'd split up and gone uphill. Jackson cursed himself that they hadn't started the search outdoors sooner.

After a fruitless search, he'd gone home. He'd taken a long, hot shower, feeling cold and sore. He'd sat on the couch watching TV but not seeing anything except that spot where they'd found blood.

Then he'd lay down on the couch and put his feet up. His eyes watched the lights on the TV until they finally drooped to a close.

Now, as he blinked owlishly in confusion, he wondered what had woken him up. Then it came again. A loud pounding at the door.

But it was so late.

Jackson swung his bare feet down and shivered when they hit the cold floor. At some point, he must have removed his shirt. But he still wore his jeans. He went to his door and checked the peephole.

It was Mazy. Instantly, he felt alarmed. He could tell through the small peephole that Mazy was a mess. He forgot all his self-deprecation and opened the door. He was no longer thinking about his complete lack of judgment in the past when he saw her.

"Jackson," Mazy gasped. She threw herself into his arms.

"Mazy!" Jackson gasped. He shut and locked the door quickly to keep the whipping wind out. "Are you okay?"

Mazy shook her head against his chest and wrapped her arms tighter around him.

Jackson took a few steps backward until they were at the sofa. He was all too aware that this was a spot where they'd made love multiple times. He forced himself to put that thought aside. He sat down and pulled her down with him, allowing her to snuggle into his side.

"What's happening? Are you safe?" Jackson glanced toward

the door, half expecting someone to burst in after her.

"I'm scared, Jackson. So scared." Her words came out muffled, but he heard every one of them.

"Hey, honey, what are you scared of?" he asked.

"I can't—I just want you to hold me."

"Well, Mazy, if you won't tell me what's happening, I can't help you. It would be so much better if you prepared me for—"

Mazy didn't let him finish his sentence. Instead, she was kissing him. She threw off her jacket but started shivering, despite her thick cable knit sweater. Her hands were caressing his bare chest. Jackson gently took her cold hands in his own, pulled back from her kiss, and looked into her eyes.

"I've missed you, Mazy. God knows how much. But can we just slow down and talk?" he asked.

"I can't Jackson. I'm in deep. I just want, no need, your strong arms around me. Just for one more night. I'm going away tomorrow. Can you just love me for one more night before everything changes?"

Jackson was speechless. He felt emotionally drained. He was physically spent.

"Mazy, I'm exhausted. I had just fallen asleep when you knocked." Jackson ran a hand through his wild, still damp hair. "As strange as this may sound, will you just come sleep with me —actually sleep? I'm not sure what tomorrow will bring either, but tonight, I can promise you a nice, warm bed."

Mazy placed a trembling hand in Jackson's. Jackson led her to his bedroom and into his bed. Mazy cuddled up next to him and Jackson was asleep in minutes. Sometime in the night, Mazy shed her sweater and jeans. Jackson was vaguely aware of her body against his as he slept and knew he talked fitfully in his sleep. It was a habit of his.

A thought flit through his mind before he fell soundly into a slumber.

Don't trust your feelings, Jackson. You can't trust yourself with her.

51

JACKSON

Jackson woke feeling disoriented. He was in his bed. But he wasn't alone. He could hear a muffled sound coming from the other side of the bed. Then it came back to him. He'd invited Mazy in last night and had fallen asleep.

He rolled over and gently placed a hand on her bare shoulder. He had no recollection of anything other than sleep. Her body was shaking. It was then that he realized she was crying.

"Hey, Mazy," Jackson whispered softly. "What's wrong?"

"I—I can't," she sighed.

Jackson put his hand around her small body and snugged her up against him, enjoying the way they fit together. Her skin felt cool against his. He buried his face in her silky hair and took in her light vanilla scent.

"I can protect you," he heard his own voice say, still thick from sleep.

"There's nothing you, or I, can do. It's too late," her voice sounded hopeless.

Jackson felt his alarm increase. Feeling more awake, Jackson put his arms around her protectively. "Hey, Mazy. Tell me what's going on. What's too late? What's happened?"

Mazy turned her body to face his and looked into his eyes. "There are some things neither you, nor I, can control. Please, can we just be together tonight? No matter what happens tomorrow, we can pretend this is our forever after."

"Mazy, you're scaring me—" Jackson's words were cut off when Mazy's warm mouth found his.

Jackson's head swam as warmth surged through his body. Mazy's hands found their way into his hair. His hands moved to her body. He lightly brushed over her side and around to her back where he unsnapped her bra. She shrugged it off and let it fall to the floor. He continued his movement until his hands were gently tracing the fullness of her breasts.

Mazy moaned quietly. "I've missed this."

Her words sped up his heart. "I've missed you."

Mazy unbuttoned his jeans. Jackson vaguely remembered falling asleep with them on earlier. She made fast work of undressing him. Her hands skimmed his inner thighs and Jackson felt himself grow hard instantly. He felt her mouth cover him, warm and soft, slow at first, then faster and faster.

"Woah," he warned. "Slow down."

Mazy shimmied out of her panties and crawled up until her body hovered just above his. She hesitated as she looked into his eyes. "Tonight, I choose you."

It was all the invitation Jackson needed. He tumbled her under him, his body on top of hers and with all the restraint he could muster, he entered her slowly. Mazy gasped with instant pleasure and arched her back to meet him. Jackson increased his rhythm until he felt her hot, wet release. He sped up until he, too, felt release and moaned in pleasure. When they finished together, he collapsed against her. He held her close, his heart racing, fear creeping in.

She was leaving in the morning. She had said as much. But Jackson never wanted her to leave again.

"Don't leave," he commanded gently.

"I can't stay," she said. "I'm a part of something. It's become bigger than me."

"Whatever has happened, it's not too late. We can fix it. Together."

"Don't ask me to choose. I can't," she replied.

"Choose what?"

"It's you or her. I can't have you both."

Jackson stiffened. "Mazy, whatever it is. You can tell me."

"Murder," she said softly. "I tried to stop it. But it was too late."

Jackson pulled Mazy into his arms. His heart was beating fast. "I won't make you choose," he promised.

"Good," Mazy said, her eyes dropping back to sleep.

In the morning, Mazy left him.

52

MINA

Mina had been on her way out of town when she'd gotten the call that stopped her. From the one person—the only person—who could get her attention.

"Please don't leave me, Mina. Not like this," Mazy's sad, soft voice reminded her of the night Mina had killed her dad and ran. The night Mazy had made Mina take her with her.

"Mazy, I don't have time. I have to go. Now!" Mina's voice was resolute. She tried to fluff her hair. Truth be told, she felt a little insecure about seeing anyone right now. She'd stayed in a hotel last night but she had left all her hair products and makeup at home. She was as natural as it got despite the fact that she was still wearing yesterday's office attire—a black sweater, black leather pants, and high-heel leather boots.

"Please," Mazy's voice came again. "I just want to say goodbye."

Mina agreed. They met where they always had when times had gotten tough over the years. An old, abandoned playground on top of a hill where they could see the city and far off into the distance. They could see for miles.

Mazy was there before her, standing on the hilltop, looking

sad. Tragic but beautiful. Like the heroine of an old classic drama—Mazy's hair was slicked back in a low ponytail, though several strands had managed to escape and whipped around her face. She was bundled in a long, brown peacoat with skinny jeans and brown boots that snugged up around her legs and over her knees.

Mina climbed the gentle slope and found herself in front of Mazy.

The wind was chilling as it raged around them. A furious wind that felt like the emotions stirring inside Mina and Mazy. Mina knew this because Mazy often felt the same way Mina did. At least, that was what Mazy always said.

Mazy stood a foot from Mina, her arms wrapped protectively across her body. Mina wasn't sure if Mazy was trying to protect herself from the wind or from Mina. There was no hiding who Mina was anymore. No more manipulating Mazy. Mazy had seen what Mina was capable of. It felt like something important was about to end.

"Well?" Mina asked defiantly. "You must have tracked me down for a reason."

"I didn't want to end things the way we did the other day," Mazy's eyes showed uncertainty.

"The day you left me when I needed you the most?" Mina challenged. She knew her words sounded like an older sister bullying the younger. Mazy really had been a sister to her.

Mazy shook her head, finding strength from somewhere within. "I left you because I could no longer be involved in this plan of yours. You went too far, Mina."

"What did you think was going to happen, Mazy? You were there the night I came up with this plan. You held me while I cried over Ludwig. You cried with me. I saw you. Your heart was as broken as mine." Tears filled Mina's eyes as she remembered that day over a year ago when Mazy had tracked her down in her worst state. Paige had killed Ludwig Lacose, killing Mina's one chance for happiness. Mina needed revenge. Mina would take her revenge on Paige so she could feel at peace. She'd sobbed all over Mazy who had held her and agreed with what must have sounded like incoherent babbling.

Shh, yes, yes, of course. Revenge is just what you need... Mazy had cooed softly.

"I don't know," Mazy now admitted, her eyes flitting to the side as she seemed to be searching for the answer. "I think I just wanted to hear you that night and acknowledge your pain."

"But you took the police services job!" Mina's voice pitched up. "You agreed to help be my eyes and ears in case my plan blew up in my face."

Mazy shrugged. "I needed a job, Mina. To be honest, I didn't actually think I'd get the job. Your recommendation cinched it. They thought you were a god there. And you didn't exactly share the kidnapping part of your plan."

"Unbelievable! You promised me. We promised each other. We would always have each other's backs. No matter what," Mina stomped a heeled boot for emphasis.

"*No matter what* didn't include murder," Mazy whispered. The wind carried her words to Mina.

Mina felt like she'd been slapped.

"Did you kill them?" Mazy asked. "Did you kill Eric and Vanessa?"

Mina nodded slowly.

"And that man at the apartment, you killed him too?" Mazy asked.

Mina nodded again. "He knew too much. He wanted to blackmail me."

Mazy sucked in air. She had started to shake, and Mina didn't think it was due to the weather. Strands of Mazy's black hair whipped around her face, momentarily blocking her view. She tucked some strands around her ear. "Do you know where James is?"

Mina shook her head.

"Do the cops know?" Mazy asked.

Mina shrugged and shook her head again. "I don't know what they know. He disappeared. After you left, the sirens showed up. I rolled James down the hill. I went back inside. When I went back out that night to look for him, he was gone."

Mazy's eyes flicked downhill and behind Mina.

Mina whirled around in time to see a truck pull into the parking lot at the bottom of the hill. Jackson exited the vehicle along with Stephen Wilton and another man. She turned back to Mazy in a panic.

"You ratted!" Mina accused, her eyes full of surprise and disappointment.

"Not to them," Mazy said sadly, "but I'm not surprised they're here. I assumed Jackson would follow me."

"So that's it then?" Mina spat angrily. "You chose him over me. After all we've been through?'

"I agreed with your choice to kill your dad, Mina. You were my hero in that moment. I didn't have the courage to kill the man who was abusing me. Then you helped me escape my terrible life and *him*. You were my hero then too. I really felt like I owed you. But this... this is too far. I can't be a part of this."

Mina lifted her chin defiantly. She knew the men were closing in. She had nowhere to run.

"Mina Martin?" Stephen's voice sounded over the wind. "Don't move. I've pulled my gun. I don't want to shoot you." There were three of them. Stephen Wilton, J. Jackson, and the officer who had escorted Mina home, though she couldn't remember his name.

"You're under arrest," the officer announced.

Mina put her hands up, but her eyes stayed trained on Mazy. "I hope you enjoy every day of your freedom," Mina said for Mazy's ears only. "God forbid you ever make a mistake. Because I'd hate to think about who you'll call when I'm locked away."

Stephen had reached Mina. "You have the right to remain silent. Anything you say can and will be used against you..."

Mina tuned him out. Her eyes held Mazy's eyes. Mazy's eyes flicked toward the parking lot and back again.

A single tear leaked out of Mazy's eye. Then another and another, until she was crying so hard she had a hard time catching her breath.

Mina hardened her heart. "I don't regret it," she told Mazy. "Not one single action."

"Mina, where's James?" Jackson asked.

Mina was obstinately silent.

"You know the drill, Mina. If you cooperate, it will go better for you," Jackson said.

"That's just something we used to tell criminals to get them talking," Mina smiled broadly as she turned to face Jackson. "Ask her. Your *girlfriend*. She knows the whole story. But I will only talk to my lawyer from here on out."

In the distance, car doors slammed. Two men dressed in black got out of a black, unmarked car.

Stephen quickly pulled Mina's hands behind her back and handcuffed her. He pulled Mina close, keeping his gun still trained on her while they all watched two men climb the gently sloping hill. Both men were fit. One was a couple inches taller than the other. Otherwise, they were similar with crew cuts and black duster jackets.

"RCMP, sorry we're late," said one of the men as he approached the group. He was the tall one. He had light stubble on his chin. His partner was shorter and a bit stockier. Both had dark hair and plain faces. They stopped in front of Mina.

"Who the hell are you?" Stephen sputtered.

"Royal Canadian Mounted Police," Jackson supplied. "They're like the FBI of Canada."

"Who is that?" Stephen asked.

Now, Mina felt scared. "RCMP trumps police services. Typically when they want to shut down organized crime, a ring of crimes, or a serial killer, these guys show up." It was in that moment Mina realized she might be in more trouble than she initially thought.

Nobody moved.

Finally, the taller RCMP officer reached out for Mina. "We'll take it from here. Good work, guys. We've been tracking her and thought she was going to get out of town before we had the chance to bring her in."

"Hold on," Jackson protested. "How about you show us your badges?"

Both men produced legitimate IDs.

Jackson sighed deeply. He stepped aside and let the men take Mina.

"This isn't how this was supposed to go," Mazy spoke up. Her face was red from crying. "Wait!"

The men stopped walking.

Mazy ran to Mina and folded her into a hug.

Mina stiffened. Even if her hands weren't cuffed, she would not have hugged Mazy back. She knew the truth now. Mazy had sold her out for her own freedom. Mina knew everything there was to know about Mazy. Even if Mazy didn't know she knew.

Mina sidestepped out of Mazy's embrace and walked a few steps. Then she turned and looked over her shoulder at Mazy who stood still crying while she watched Mina go. This would be the last time she saw the woman who she had once called *sister*.

"You're dead to me." Mina turned angrily and walked away.

53

JAMES

"James! Thank God!" Stephen Wilton burst through the hospital room as if he was about to free me from a hostage situation.

"At ease, man." I couldn't help but chuckle. It hurt a little though. My shoulder sported a large bandage, and my arm was in a sling. I remembered very little from the last twenty-four hours. I had been brought in unconscious. Dumped here, actually.

A nurse told me later that I had woken, delirious before the post-op sedation kicked in, and told her the name of my wife and rattled off Paige's phone number a few times. That's how they were able to track down my insurance information before my surgery.

"What in the world happened to you, James?" Stephen asked. "We've been looking everywhere for you. We arrested Mina Martin and we do have the footage from the airport showing she picked you up. But that's not a crime. We won't be able to hold her unless we can prove she did something wrong. We have no evidence."

"Oh, she did something wrong alright," I quipped. I could

only smile about it now because it was over. "She kidnapped me from the airport, held me in a room for a few days. She killed two people—one I heard and the other one she confessed to—then shot me when I managed to escape. I somehow rolled down a hill away from her. That part is fuzzy.

"What I do remember is I awoke suddenly, my whole body jerked as if I had been falling. When I opened my eyes, I instantly felt pain radiating from every part of my body. It hadn't been a dream like I'd thought it had been. The last thing I remembered before I hit the ground—though vaguely—was falling.

"When I came to, I remembered thinking, if I'd somehow gotten away from Mina by falling down this hill, it meant I was free. I recall the adrenaline that shot through my body at that thought. I raised my head to look around, but everything was spinning. So, I put my head back down and closed my eyes. From what I could see, I was alone. But I wasn't okay. I took deep breaths while attempting to take inventory. My body, while shaking, felt hot and sweaty. My shoulder was numb. My head was pounding.

"I felt myself pass out again. The next thing I know, I felt like I was flying. I was moving, but I wasn't moving myself. That part is still a mystery. Someone carried me, put me in a car, and transported me—somewhere. I was in and out of consciousness. The only time I almost gained consciousness, they shot me with drugs that knocked me out again. I thought I'd been kidnapped again. They must have dropped me at the ER. But when I asked who brought me in, I got blank looks. No one saw them. They didn't sign in or leave a name.

"I think I woke up on a bed being wheeled into a room. I gave them Paige's name and number, then passed out," I finished. I felt tired and emotional from telling that story.

Stephen shook his head in disbelief. "That's when Paige called me. We had a police services officer post up outside your room to make sure your kidnapper, or rescuer, didn't return for you. And they called me when you were out of surgery. But we got a little distracted arresting Mina."

"Nice," I put my good hand up to high-five Stephen.

Stephen grinned and pointed to my shoulder. "What's going on there?"

"A little bone grafting, a few screws and a few pins to put my bones back in place. They had to repair some of the soft tissue —ligaments and tendons and such. But the good news is they didn't have to do a joint replacement."

Stephen shuddered. "Did they have to remove the bullet?"

"They didn't have to. It had been pulled out before I got here. The force of the shot did a lot of damage. They told me removing the bullet wasn't enough to fix me." I was matter of fact about this. Guys on the police force gave respect for such wounds like gunshots.

Stephen nodded his approval. "So, you feel up to giving a statement against Mina Martin? Then we can get you on a plane to go home."

Now I felt worried. "Can you see any way this could go wrong? I really need to get home to my wife." Having talked to Paige after the anesthetic wore off, I discovered the babies were coming early. They would be here any day.

"Considering that we finally got the airport footage, and she's in a jail cell, I'm going to say you're safe. Your testimony will tie this up. We'll need it before we put you on a plane. She'll be in prison for life. It'll be all finished."

I nodded. "Count me in then. On the condition that I never have to come back here again."

"I'm with you there, my friend." Stephen shook my good hand.

"What's next for you, Stephen?" I asked.

"I'll continue my search for Demitri Abbott," he answered, looking serious.

I lowered my voice, matching his tone, feeling protective over my bonus daughter. "I hope you find that son of a bitch. Sooner, rather than later."

"You and me both, James," Stephen agreed.

"If anyone can do it, you can, Stephen."

54

JACKSON

"Fill in the gaps for me, Mazy. What happened?" Jackson asked. They were sitting in the diner where they'd fallen in love the day they were both fired from the force.

Mazy looked beautiful and at peace, having showered and slept. She looked more casual than ever in jeans, knee-high boots, and a white sweater. Her hair was pulled back into a low ponytail. Despite her restful state, there was a sadness in her eyes that would take a long time to heal.

In response to Jackson's question, Mazy fiddled with the edge of the tablecloth. She looked in Jackson's eyes.

"No secrets," she said as if she was talking to herself more than anyone else. "Mina and I met when we were barely older than teenagers. We lived in Alaska at the time. I still feel I owe her a debt. She took me away from someone who was hurting me."

Jackson reached out, his eyes soft, as he caressed Mazy's hand.

"We came here, to Winnipeg. We built separate lives. Mina, as you know, got a job with the police services and was thriving. I was not. It was only a matter of time before I got in with a group of people who made a living stealing things and turning them in to the big boss." Mazy's fingers made air quotes over the words *big boss*.

"Then I got caught. Only, it wasn't considered a petty crime and it wasn't the police. Mina had helped me out of a scrape or two in the past. This time, it was Royal Canadian Mounted Police—"

"RCMP," Jackson said, making the connection between what happened on the hill and where this story was leading. "I'm surprised they cared about theft."

"They didn't. They cared about the boss. They asked me to turn on him. They said he was a dangerous criminal, and they'd been looking for him a long time. They said I was lucky to be alive. They really scared me. They said it was only a matter of time before he killed me or pulled me in further to his crime ring."

"What did you do?" Jackson asked, hanging on every word.

"I flipped. I got them the evidence they wanted. He's still locked up. I thought that would be the end of it. My get-outta-jail-free card."

"It wasn't?" Jackson asked.

Mazy shook her head. "No. They wanted me to be an informant. Their eyes and ears. I swear, they should have paid me for the information I've given them over the years—"

"I'm surprised you turned on Mina though," Jackson interrupted.

Mazy bristled and looked sad again. "Right, Mina. Well, when she vacated the police services job, RCMP wanted me to fill it. They loved the idea, since there had been a dirty cop in the department. Mina wanted me to take the job to divert police away from her if they decided to look into her. They were all using me. I was so tired of it. I wanted to throw it all out the window and run away with you."

"You did?" Jackson asked, feeling surprised.

"Don't act like you didn't know! The perfume, the clothes I wore, my perfect hair with every piece in perfect place. I did that for you."

"You did?" Jackson was dumbfounded.

"Anyway, I wanted out. I wanted all of them to leave me alone, so I looked for an opportunity and eventually came up with the plan."

"Did you know Mina had James?"

Mina shook her head, her ponytail swishing back and forth. "Not at first. I mean, I was the only one who was there to comfort her when she was devastated over this guy she'd been seeing. He had been murdered."

"Lacose." Jackson shook his head, trying to wrap his brain around it. "Lacose and Mina."

Mazy nodded. "Well, Mina wanted revenge. I didn't know the guy was Lacose. I didn't even know who Lacose was. Even if I did, I wouldn't have connected the story to James. But when you started talking about Lacose, I started snooping through the system more, and I started to put things together."

"When did you know what Mina had done?" Jackson asked.

"The night she called me and said she had a situation. I knew she had killed someone before—"

"She did?" Jackson was horrified. Had he missed Mina's criminal activity when he worked with her at the station as well?

"Yes, she killed her dad. That's why we left Alaska that night. It was self-defense. He practically killed her mom and went after her too. I applauded her. She was my hero. But a few nights ago, when she called me, I was terrified with what I saw when I got there."

"What did you see?" he asked.

"She had just killed a random guy who caught her in the act—"

"What act?"

"James had broken out. Before he got away, she shot him. She was trying to get him back to the apartment which is why she called me. She was desperate and I always help her if I can."

"But you didn't know she had kidnapped James?"

"No, I didn't. Not at that point. So I get there. There's this dead guy in the woods and James, who was bleeding profusely from the shot in the shoulder. I helped her pick James up, processing and trying to make sense of what was happening. The more Mina said and the more agitated she seemed with me, the more I understood. I dropped James and stopped helping. About that time, I heard sirens."

"What did you do?"

"I went to my car and called RCMP. I saw my opportunity to get free of all of them. I promised to give them Mina in exchange for freedom. They agreed and asked me to watch Mina. So, I did. From a distance."

"And then?" Jackson asked.

"I helped them get James back to their headquarters. They promised to release me after that. They lied. They made me stay while they attempted to question James. They needed to know what he knew. They wanted to make sure he wasn't involved with Mina in a different capacity than what I perceived. They didn't know his body would be in shock. He'd lost so much blood and hit his head. He was so weak. They called in the travel surgeon who could only do so much. She removed the bullet but, in the end, they had to take him to ER."

"Were they able to question him?" Jackson asked.

"Barely. They kept him sedated and kept dosing him with this drug they called truth serum." Mazy snorted as if she'd heard a joke. "I thought it was all bunk. Until barely conscious James started answering the questions. Turns out, *truth serum* is really barbiturates."

"Did you know the things James talked about?" Jackson wondered.

"No. He said Mina had taken him to avenge Lacose's death. She needed to get Paige here so she could watch it all go down," Mazy shuddered.

Jackson patted her hand.

"You think you know someone… But Mina had changed. She wasn't herself when I saw her the other day," said Mazy.

"What do you mean?" asked Jackson.

"Her eyes. They were brown, but when I was with her, they had turned black. She was cold—colder than normal—and emotionless. Her movements were different as well. It's hard to explain. They were jerky and almost—"

"What?" Jackson felt impatient to know.

"Masculine. Like she had been—"

"Possessed?" Jackson finished.

"Do you believe in that sort of thing?" Mazy asked. She looked fearful.

"No," Jackson said quickly. Chills ran over him.

"Me neither," Mazy agreed. She raised a sweater sleeve to reveal goosebumps on her arm. "Still, it's hard to fathom how out of control Mina got in the end."

"And all her murder victims were killed in the exact way Lacose had killed Jessup. That seems a little too coincidental…"

Both stared at each other, feeling horrified over the implications. Either Mina had become the exact replica of Lacose, or the ghost of Lacose had possessed Mina's body to finish, from the grave, what he'd started before his death—revenge.

55

JAMES

Aurora and Austin Friesen were born at 12:50 a.m. on October 25. I had slipped into the delivery room just in time to see Aurora born. Austin was not far behind his sister.

"You made it," Paige said in an exhale as they placed a baby in her arms.

"Dad, would you like to hold the other one?" the nurse asked after she measured and weighed the baby.

"Would I?" I asked, my heart racing in my chest. The nurse carefully placed Austin in my arms, arranging him so I could grasp him with my good arm and balance him with the part of my arm that wasn't in the sling. I thought I would burst with pride. Instead, my eyelids burst. Tears ran unchecked down my cheeks and came so quickly, for a minute, I couldn't see. My life would never be the same. The amount of gratitude I felt holding my child, when one week ago, I didn't know if I would live another day.

I didn't tell Paige the amount of sprinting and running through airports I'd done just to maneuver getting home when I did. Stephen was a huge help, of course. It's harder to run with an arm in a sling than I would've thought possible.

We'd gotten the text from Paige that she was heading to the hospital again just as we'd stepped off the plane in Missouri. But I'd made it. That's all that mattered in this moment. I'd made it here in time and alive.

"Where's Anna?" I asked. "She needs to meet her siblings."

Paige smiled. Her eyes were tired but happy. "She's with Brandi Burnett. Out in the lobby."

I took a step toward the door, Austin still snuggled into my arms. He'd put his fist up to his forehead like he was shielding his eyes from the bright light. I smiled, wondering if I could love anyone any more than him in this moment.

"Sir, you can't take the baby with you," the nurse said sternly.

"Oops, of course," I grinned broadly. This was my boy, but I was confined to the room with him. Soon enough I'd take him home. For now, I wasn't willing to leave him. "Maybe we can text Brandi to bring Anna in?"

"Yeah," Paige said softly as she patted the bed. "There's room right here."

She didn't have to ask me twice. I hurried to her side. I gazed at Aurora who was staring up at her mother with a look of wonderment on her face. She was miraculous. I'd always wanted kids of my own and now I had two. I was alive. I was reunited with my beautiful wife. I had two healthy babies and a bonus daughter who took that moment to burst into the room.

"Daddy James!" Anna shrieked as she came to hug my leg. "You're home!"

"That's right, princess," I greeted her. With my arms full, it was hard to hug her back. I found a chair and sat down.

Anna peered into Austin's face. "Oh! He has no hair! Where's his hair?"

I laughed. "It'll grow."

"What's this?" Anna jabbed at my sling and shoulder wrapping.

"Anna, be careful with his shoulder," Paige said quietly.

"Oh, I fell down a hill," I told the half-truth with a pang. I wanted honesty in all areas of my life, but I thought telling Anna I'd been shot would lead to more questions. Not to mention, Paige didn't even know the full story yet.

"Where's the other baby?" Anna asked.

"Mom's got her," I said.

Anna bounced over to Paige's bed. She climbed up in the bed where Paige had made room for me a minute ago. As she had with her brother, she peered down into Aurora's face. She gently kissed the baby's forehead.

"She's looking right at me!" Anna said excitedly.

"She recognizes your voice," Paige said.

"She does?" Anna asked.

"Yes, babies can hear voices inside mama's tummy. You did," Paige said.

"Really?" Anna asked.

"Yes, you were crying when you were born but when I talked to you, you quieted right down and listened to me."

"Now she's looking at you!" Anna cried with glee.

"You are going to be the best big sister," Paige announced.

I got up and joined them.

"Yep, I am," Anna said. "Can I hold one?"

I gently placed Austin in Anna's arms but stayed close to supervise should Austin get wiggly, or Anna lose her grip.

I looked at all of them. My little family all huddled together on this bed at the start of what I knew would be a new, enhanced life.

The End

ALSO BY ADDISON MICHAEL

A Mynart Mystery Thriller series is ghostly suspense with psychological elements. If you like complex heroines, paranormal twists and turns, and gripping suspense, then you'll love Addison Michael's dark glimpse into the psyche. Tap the links to buy these books today!

Book 1 - *What Comes Before Dawn* - A tragic death too close to home. A young woman seeking answers. But will the truth prove fatal?

Book 2 - *Dawn That Brings Death* - Two men are dead at the Mynart Murder House. Paige, a newly single mom, is hiding in Canada. Will she be able to keep her daughter safe when a new enemy emerges?

Book 3 - *Truth That Dawns* - When Paige's secrets are exposed, she must face the consequences including a serial killer looking for revenge. He'll stop at nothing. Will Paige live to see her daughter again?

Book 4 - *Dawn That Breaks* - Anna is gone. It starts with a deadly car accident that creates too many questions. Will Paige learn the truth about her daughter, Anna, *before* a deadly ghost from her past ends Paige's life?

The Other AJ Hartford - A phantom on a train. A mysterious kidnapping long ago. Can she connect the dots before all her futures disappear forever? If you like good-hearted heroines, ghostly phenomena, and nail-biting high stakes, then you'll love Addison Michael's mind-blowing adventure. Tap the link to buy the book today!

Join the Addison Michael Newsletter to receive the FREE story *How it Began*!

REVIEW REQUEST

If you enjoyed this book, I would be extremely grateful if you would leave a brief review on the store site where you purchased your book or on Goodreads. Your review helps fellow readers know what to expect when they read this book.

~ Addison Michael

ABOUT THE AUTHOR

 Addison Michael writes riveting, character-driven stories heavy in suspense with a focus on the intriguing motivations that make a person a murderer.

Addison grew up in a home where rules were not meant to be broken. As such, she was the "goodest" of the "goody two shoes" around. Being the oldest of six siblings forced Addison to lead by example. Her golden reputation solidified well into her thirties.

But every good girl needs to have an outlet. Behind every smile and sweet comment, there is a dark side waiting to emerge. Addison Michael found the outlet for her dark side writing thrillers. She has an uncanny ability to step outside herself and create believable characters who navigate unbelievable circumstances involving murder, mystery, secrets, and suspense.

Made in United States
Orlando, FL
07 March 2024

44496663R00134